DEADLY RUSE

Only instinct warned Ry Buckner. He turned in his saddle and saw Sam Tull on hands and knees scuttling to where moonlight winked from his thrown six-shooter. He knew then that Tull had pretended to be worse hurt than he'd been, wanting, probably, a few more moments to gather his strength. He saw Tull grasp the gun and bring it up flaming. He tried reaching for his own gun too late. Something smote his left shoulder hard, the shock of that blow driving him into a daze. He reeled, sure that he was falling from the saddle. He clutched the horn.

He became dimly aware that his horse was running, and he bent all effort to one need. He must keep to the saddle while the night rushed by and a deeper darkness closed in, blinding him. . . .

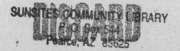

Also by Norman A. Fox

ROUGHSHOD

LONG LIGHTNING

ROPE THE WIND

THE PHANTOM SPUR

SILENT IN THE SADDLE

The Hard Pursued

NORMAN A. FOX

A Dell Book

Published by
Dell Publishing
a division of
Bantam Doubleday Dell Publishing Group, Inc.
666 Fifth Avenue
New York, New York 10103

ISBN: 0-440-21054-2

Printed in the United States of America

Published simultaneously in Canada

April 1993

10 9 8 7 6 5 4 3 2 1

RAD

Contents

1. Man Cornered   1
2. Fear by Night   15
3. Man Blocked   29
4. The Violent Ones   41
5. Gulley Loads a Gun   53
6. To the Hills   65
7. Deadlocked   79
8. Three on the Trail   91
9. Man Wounded   105
10. Truce by Moonlight   117
11. The Sleepless Ones   131
12. To the Cave   145
13. Came McQueen   157
14. The Struggle   169
15. Gulley Empties a Gun   183
16. To Hatchet   197
17. The Hangmen   209
18. Showdown at Signal   221

1 : Man Cornered

Ahead, the locomotive that had labored against mountain grade ever since Helena hooted at Signal's one-mile sign, and Riley Buckner stirred on his bed of scooped-up straw. Through the slatted sides of this empty cattle car the wind poured cold, and he wished he had a sheepskin coat. Outside, darkness rushed by, and beneath him the floor rumbled. He coughed as cinder-laden smoke billowed back. Fine riding for a saddleman! But outside, too, were lifts of land dimly discerned in the night, and he was sure he smelled pine and spruce; and by faint moonlight he glimpsed the high-piled contour of Table Mountain. Homesickness caught at his throat then, and his five years' absence was bridged. But Table Mountain brought back Duke Jordan and the cave and all the things they had done as boys. And the insistent question arose: how did he really feel about Duke?

Soon now he'd know, he hoped. He was his own man again, free to think, free to act. That had been the real hell of prison, he decided, being told when to eat and where to sleep and what to do with the hours between, so that when he finally got pushed outside, he felt forsaken. Forsaken and adrift until he'd latched onto the idea that put him riding this rattler back to Signal. He had to stand in the courtroom again. That was it. When you lost a thing—be it a horse or a mood or a friendship—you went to the place where you'd lost it. He would go to where he'd last seen Duke.

Trouble was, when he put his mind to Duke, too many other people got into his thinking. Duke's dad, old Gulley Jordan, for instance. And Larkin Rigby of Hatchet ranch, enemy to the Jordans and therefore one-time enemy to Riley Buckner. And Dorcas Lane, who had sometimes been his girl and sometimes Duke's, with no ill feeling between them on that account. These people, too, had been in the courtroom that last day. But his real concern was with Duke. Get his thinking straight about Duke, and he would know where to aim his life now that he had the aiming in his own hands again.

He arose from the straw. He had no belongings to gather. He hauled back the car door and leaned into the night as the lights of Signal slid into view below him. The train crawled the bench above town, the mountains loomed around big and familiar, and the huddled buildings of Signal lay formless in the depth of the gulch and along its slopes. He looked for the huge bulk of the courthouse and thought he made it out.

The freight slowed. There was a siding up here on the bench, and he supposed they were stopping to cut out a car or two. He leaned farther out and saw the engine abreast of the depot. Vague shapes stood beneath the eaves, but he had business with no man in Signal; and with the depot still a hundred yards away and the train still moving, he made his jump.

He hit the embankment and rolled and lost his hat. He picked himself up and went searching for it, clambering up the pitch. He saw four men move from the depot platform and come toward him along the welt of the grade, running in single file beside the string of freight cars. "There he is!" one shouted, the sound nearly lost beneath the clash of couplings as the train jarred to a stop. "Head him off! He's trying to get aboard!"

He picked up his hat and put it on. He had no reason to run from these men; neither did he care to be recognized. Surely they hadn't made out his face at such a distance by night. They had simply made a mistake. They had been waiting for someone leaving town, and they had not seen him jump but had spied him climbing and so assumed he was their man. But there was no chance to escape. The four of them were upon him, leaping at him and bearing him down.

He fought back, having no choice. He got his arms around a couple of them, and they went tumbling together down the embankment, the other two following and adding their weight to the pile at the bottom. He struck out hard, wringing a grunt from one, a curse from another. They pinioned his arms and hauled him to his feet. One peered into his face and said in disgust, "We got the wrong man! It's Ry Buckner come back!"

He recognized all four now, hands from Lark Rigby's Hatchet outfit—big Rufe York, Heck Lund, the two Darby brothers. Tough men, all, and none too bright.

He'd had his rounds with each of them at one time and another when he'd ridden for Gulley Jordan's Boxed J. "All right, boys," he said. "You made a mistake. Now get your hands off me."

He tried squirming free. One of the Darbys let go of him, but Rufe York said, "I don't know about this. We'd better take him to Spence. Spence might want to talk to him."

Astonished, Buckner said, *"Spence?* Since when has *Spence* Rigby done the talking for Hatchet?"

"Never you mind," York said. "Come along now."

They let go of him, but they kept him pocketed. He looked from one to another and then shrugged. It was come along or fight, with the matter not worth fighting about. They started on down the slope and soon were among the outskirt dwellings. Thus he came home.

He supposed there should be some response in him to that. He'd been five when he'd first hit Signal, so he'd known no other town really. He had seen Signal first as a mining town, and there were many a deserted shaft in the hills and many a mound marking some prospect hole to speak of the golden glory that was gone. Later he'd known Signal as a cowtown, and in the sweeping valley to the west cattle still ranged. He could name every occupant in the dark houses among which they now threaded, save for the changes of the five years, which would be few. Good folks, all of them, but lost to him now, he supposed.

Like Dorcas. They had turned into an alley and were passing the high board fence behind Maw Lane's place, the old frame structure the widow had bought when her general store had attained something approximating prosperity. Dorcas dwelt in that house—Dorcas and her sister Pru and the widow, their mother. Remembering, his pulse leaped. He wanted to ask about Dorcas, but not of these men. He didn't realize that he had stopped until one of them pushed him.

"Keep movin'," the fellow said.

At the alley's far end they came to the back door of a building which he knew was the Frontier Bar. That fitted. Spence Rigby owned the place. But the rest of it still didn't make sense—Spence commanding service from Hatchet hands.

The door opened to a small room blue with tobacco smoke and sour with the smell of the beer kegs piled along one wall. A roll-top desk against another wall made this an office. Two men were here. They sat at a round table, the shade drawn on the one window, a lamp burning on the table, and a map of the county spread before them. Buckner knew both men. They were Spence Rigby and Sam Tull, Hatchet foreman. They looked up, showing surprise.

"Ry Buckner!" Rigby said and stood up, hand extended. "Home from stony lonesome, huh? We heard you were out, but that was a month ago. Began to figure you weren't coming back here."

Buckner looked straight at Rigby and ignored the proffered hand. Rigby had put on weight, he saw; the man had too much belly sagging over his cartridge belt and too much bourbon flush on his round, wide-mouthed face. Spence must be pushing forty-five now. Gambler's black only made him look gross, and the string tie seemed to choke him.

"What's on your mind, Spence?" he asked.

Rigby let his hand fall but kept his smile. "Benchmade boots," he observed. "Probably out of a second-hand store, but good ones. Pants, shirt, coat, hat —the kind a rider would wear. You did yourself pretty proud, Ry, on the ten dollars they gave you when they let you through the big gate."

"If it's any of your business," Buckner said, "I worked a month in Helena after I left Deer Lodge. It gave me a stake."

"Come in on the freight tonight?"

Rufe York, standing behind Buckner, said, "He must 'a' jumped from one of the cars. We figgered him to be climbin' on when we spotted him, though. Same height and frame. Nobody tried makin' that train, Spence. We wasted our time. We're wastin' more now. Why ain't we hittin' saddles?"

"Soon, Rufe," Rigby said. "Soon."

Buckner said, "Rufe thought we should palaver. He was wrong. I've got nothing to say to you."

Rigby shook his head. "Things have changed, Ry. No need of that chip on your shoulder. I could use you, and I reckon you could use a job. How you feeling about Duke Jordan these days?"

He saw the eagerness in Rigby's squinted eyes. Duke Jordan—? He could guess now how the mistake had been made at the depot. "Same height and frame," Rufe York had said. Duke and he were both six-foot-two and of the same broad-shouldered, lean-hipped build. Could have been Duke they thought they'd seen. But Duke didn't hop freights, and even if he chose to do so, why would Hatchet be trying to stop him?

Spence Rigby's question still hung in the air. He

frowned at Rigby. How could he say how he felt about Duke Jordan when he didn't truly know himself? "I was Duke's best friend," he said. "Maybe I'm still his best friend."

Rigby snorted. "After Boxed J put you in the pen?"

"Look, Spence, I haven't got all night to stand here jawing," he said. "So I'm going to spell it out slow and plain and final. When I drew Boxed J pay, that made me an enemy of Hatchet. I sided the Jordans against Lark Rigby in their squabbles over that strip of land between them. That was one thing. You were another. When I left here, Lark wasn't speaking to you, his own brother. He had the same measure of you that everybody had—a cheap saloonman selling watered whiskey and fleecing cowboys with marked decks. If you and Lark have made peace since and he's taken you in as some kind of partner, that's his bad luck. But I want no part of you or any proposition you've got to make."

Still Spence Rigby smiled, but the whiskey flush had gone from his face, leaving it ashy gray. In the sudden silence, a dozen distant sounds came clear—the talk of men, the click of poker chips, the beat of a piano in the barroom, the scuff of a horse's hoofs as someone rode the street, the chuffing of the train above town where cars were being switched. Rigby sat down at the table. His voice came harsh. "You're making a mistake," he said. "A very bad mistake."

"I'll try living with it," Buckner said. He turned toward the door. Big Rufe York looked toward Rigby. Rigby nodded, and York stepped aside. So did the other three Hatchet hands. But Sam Tull spoke then, for the first time, the one word a whiplash. *"Wait!"*

Buckner saw Tull stand up, tall and lean, his features half shadowed by his hat brim so that only his slash of a mouth and his heavy nose were plain in that death mask of a face. Tull had been Hatchet foreman a long time, Buckner remembered, a tough ramrod for a tough crew. Tull said, "Spence, don't let him go!"

Rigby looked puzzled.

"By his own say so, he ain't on our side," Tull said. "By my book, that makes him against us. That freight hasn't pulled out yet, from the sound. Let's put him on it. But let's work him over first. Lumberjack style. Fist and boot. So if he gets the notion of coming back, he'll remember he shouldn't."

Rigby thought this over, and a pleased look came into his eyes. "Sam," he said slowly, "I believe you make sense."

Behind Buckner, big Rufe York grunted, and he heard the rasp of a bootsole on the floor. He knew then where his only chance lay. He had six against him in this small room, with four of them between him and the alley door. He didn't lunge in that direction. They would have been expecting that. Instead, he charged straight at the table and grasped its edge and upended it against Rigby and Tull, dumping both men over backwards. The lamp crashed into darkness, not exploding into flame as he'd feared it might. Someone cursed as two of the Hatchet hands collided. Rigby's voice rose shrill from the floor. "Don't shoot, any of you! Block that door!"

Buckner could see the dim outline of the one window with its drawn shade. He jammed his hat down tight on his head, folded his arms before his face, and dived at the window. He went through it head first, landing in the alley in a tangle of shade, broken sash, and splintered glass. He got to his feet and began running in the feeble moonlight. Behind him a door banged open. Glancing back, he saw a man dimly silhouetted. He heard Spence Rigby shout, "Get around to the other end of the alley, some of you! Head him off!"

Men came tumbling through the doorway. He watched them, wanting to run but knowing that his footfalls would draw gunfire. He began walking rapidly, hugging shadows. Earlier tonight he'd wished he had a sheepskin coat; now he wished he had a six-shooter. He stopped suddenly and peered about. He had reached the fence behind Widow Lane's place. Boots beat along the alley from the Frontier; he thought he heard boots at the far end of the alley toward which he was headed. There must be a gate somewhere in the fence, but he didn't bother feeling for it. He grasped the top of the fence, pulled himself up, and slipped over the other side, dropping into the Lanes' back yard. He heard men out there in the alley.

"That you, Rufe?" One of the Darby brothers speaking. "Did he get by you?"

"He never got out of this alley."

Another came running up, halted. "He must have cut into somebody's yard," Spence Rigby said, panting. "Spread out, boys. Comb this neighborhood fine. He's somewhere close by."

He heard them move. He began groping across the yard toward the house. The Lanes had had no dog in the old days; he hoped they had none now. He almost ran into a clothes line. He got to a corner of the house and found himself beside a window. He tried remembering the lie of the house from five years ago, and it seemed to him that the room here at the corner was Dorcas's. He listened hard. Someone fumbled at the back fence. An annoyed voice said, "Damned gate's barred from the inside."

"Give me a boost," someone else said. "I'll climb the fence."

He heard a rasping, scuffing sound. He supposed that other men might have circled around to the front of the house by now. He made his choice, putting his hand to the window and hoping desperately that it would be unlocked. The sash gave to his touch. He raised the window, eased into the room, and quietly put the window down. He made out a bed, a bureau, a night stand and saw, dimly, the girl sitting up in the bed. "Dorcas!" he whispered. "Don't scream! Whatever you do, don't scream!"

The girl said, "I keep a gun on the night stand. I've got it covering you right now. Sing out your name."

It was Dorcas's voice, but not quite. The shade of difference made the voice Pru's. He had guessed wrong about this room. "It's Ry Buckner," he said. "Hush down, Pru. I'm being hunted."

He knelt by the window and peered out. He thought he could see someone groping the yard. His eyes ached from watching. Finally there seemed to be no moving shadow, but he couldn't be sure. Behind him, it sounded as though Pru were sobbing. Poor child, he'd probably scared her half to death. Child? Let's see, she'd been about seventeen when he'd left, which made her twenty-two now. Just the same, seeing a man climbing through the window must have been a shock.

"Don't be frightened," he said softly. "I'll be leaving soon. I think they're gone now."

"I'm not frightened," she said in a choked voice. "I'm laughing. I'm trying to cover it up by keeping a corner of the blanket jammed in my mouth."

He felt utterly foolish. "It's no laughing matter," he said severely.

"Yes, it is," she said. "You begging me not to scream, when you were within a second of having the top of your head blown off."

"I thought this was Dorcas's room."

She sobered at once. "Dorcas isn't here."

"Visiting somewhere?"

She hesitated. "Let's just say she isn't here."

He peered into the yard again. He was quite sure now that whoever had climbed the fence had gone on. "Pru, I'm sorry about this," he said. "And some puzzled. I came in on the freight tonight. Hatchet hands jumped me and took me to Spence Rigby at the Frontier. Sam Tull was there. Spence seems to be speaking for Hatchet now. I take it he and Lark patched it up."

She shook her head. "Not as of this afternoon, Ry. Lark was in town. He came into our store and told Maw he couldn't be trading with us any more. For—for reasons. Spence came down the street just as Lark walked out. I saw them. They passed each other without a word."

"Then nothing adds up," he said. He pondered a moment. "Pru, is there any reason Duke Jordan should have been getting on the freight tonight?"

"None that I know of."

He grew more baffled. "Can you give me *any* idea what's going on around here?"

"I suppose anything could be happening about now," she said. "That old trouble between Hatchet and Boxed J has come to a head. Gully Jordan fenced off that wedge of land between him and Lark Rigby not long ago. You'll remember that Lark always used that strip as right-of-way when he brought his fall gather to town for shipping. Lark's said to have threatened to tear down the fence by the end of this week. That would be today. The last thing he bought from Maw was a supply of ammunition."

He turned her information over in his mind. He was worried until he remembered that Hatchet-Boxed J trouble was no longer a concern of his. He had come back for one reason only, to stand in the courtroom again, but first he had to escape Spence Rigby's men. Very carefully he raised the window. He thrust out his head and listened. All lay quiet. "So long, Pru," he said. "And thanks."

He heard a rustling of covers and turned and made out that she had climbed from bed and was drawing a wrapper over her nightgown. She came to him and laid a hand on his arm. He saw that her hair was done up in paper curlers, but in spite of that she was prettier than he'd remembered. Pretty, almost, as Dorcas.

"What brought you back here, Ry?" she asked. "What are you looking for?"

He shrugged. "Something I lost five years ago."

"Duke?" she asked.

He nodded.

"Go away, Ry," she said. "There's nothing here for you."

He had never known her to be so intense. He had remembered her only as Dorcas's kid sister, half child, half woman, usually cluttering up the parlor when a man wanted to sit of an evening with his girl. She had been nobody to him, really, but she was his friend now. She could have screamed or she could have shot, and she had done neither.

He patted her hand. "Thanks again, Pru," he said. He slipped through the window and drew the sash down behind him and moved away from the house.

2 ⋮ Fear by Night

Wind awoke Gulley Jordan, pressing hard against his old ranch-house and prowling the eaves. Or perhaps what pulled him from sleep was the long drawn out hoot of the freight train up there in the hills, heading toward Signal. In a darkness that lay thick and cold, he found himself in his parlor chair, fully clothed, a premonition of trouble so strong in him that he shuddered. "Riley!" he shouted, still half asleep. "Riley Buckner!" He came fully awake then, shaking his head in astonishment that the name had been wrung from him.

A cry for help, really, out of troubled dreaming. He frowned. In all his seventy-two years he had asked no man for help. He was feeling his age tonight, and the years were like the darkness, cold and crowding. He tried getting out of the rocker, but a blanket had been wrapped around his legs. That pesky girl, of course! Found him snoozing in the chair and fixed him up like some helpless babe and blew out the lamp and tiptoed from the room. Guess she'd meant well, though. He felt ashamed at his own annoyance.

He kicked the blanket away and began groping for the table holding the lamp. He stumbled against another of the chairs and gave it a cussing, the brief flare of temper making him his own man again. What was the matter, he wondered, that he should be growling like a bear and hearing a dirge in the wind when its only song was autumn's?

He fumbled for the lamp. Its chimney was cold; he'd been asleep for some time. Beyond the windows blackness lay, the moon lost in a cloud rack. That wind swept down off the Garnet Hills, off Table Mountain, and here in the valley it moved across the broad acres of his Boxed J. His cattle would be drifting before it, seeking the draws and coulees. Across the other ranches, too, the wind would be keening—across Oxbow and Anchor 4 and Pothook, across small spreads and big, across Lark Rigby's Hatchet.

He'd not wanted to think about Lark Rigby. He'd shut that pushing man out of his mind lately, because to think would be to act, and Duke had argued that they should let Lark have rope, thereby to hang himself. Let the lawlessness start with Hatchet, not Boxed J, Duke had said when the word had first come that Lark had demanded that the Strip fence be torn down by today. Well, Ruby County had law all right with a rawhider like Virgil McQueen wearing the sheriff's star a good many years. But that didn't mean a man shouldn't defend his own property.

Anyway, what in blazes was Duke's idea in riding out alone early this evening, and in the direction of the Strip at that? Just going to have a look around, he'd said. Young pup should have taken the crew along. Or at least said what he was really up to. Probably he'd told that girl what he'd had in mind, but nary a word for his old man. That was what smarted. Nobody told Gulley Jordan anything any more. The crew looked to Duke for orders, or even to that girl, now that she'd become bookkeeper here.

Bookkeeper! He snorted at the notion. True, the paper work piled higher each year, and he'd always been too restless for desk work, and so had Duke. But they could have got some young feller with black alpaca sleeve guards, a celluloid collar, and a head for figures. Likely they'd have to hire such anyway, once Duke and Dorcas got married. She wasn't apt to be bothering with the ledgers once she became Mrs. Duke Jordan.

That was another thing, the two of them talking about a wedding but not getting around to it. He hadn't wasted any time with Duke's mother, you bet.

From the wall with its fancy, striped paper, the crayon portrait of Lily smiled at him. He picked the lamp from the table and held it up, and the portrait came startlingly to life. Forty-three he'd been that fall he'd come to Alder Gulch, and single because he'd found no girl that hit his fancy, and he'd moved too fast across the frontier to really look for one. But he'd walked into that Virginia City hurdy-gurdy house and had one dance with Lily and told her he was taking her out of there. They'd got married that very night, and he reckoned he'd never been sorry. Mighty pretty Lily had been. That's where Duke got his good looks and maybe the weak side of him, too, but things might have been different if the fever hadn't taken Lily, leaving Duke half an orphan at eight.

Half an orphan like Riley Buckner had been.

He scowled, setting the lamp back on the table. Now how in tarnation had he come to call out Riley's name tonight? Must have been dreaming. He tried remembering the dream but could recall only the fear with which he had awakened.

Fear? Why the devil should he be afraid? He'd lived long enough to have reached the peaceful years, hadn't he? Fear should belong to the old days, to Virginia City with its Road Agent terror and no man's life safe if he had a pinch of gold in his poke. Not that he'd walked bowlegged from the dust he'd carried, but he hadn't been poor, either. He'd got to the diggings too late to stake a rich claim, but he'd had his set of carpenter tools, packed by wagon and river boat all the way from Wisconsin. He'd built sluice boxes—yes, and coffins, too—and ridden out of the gulch six months later, Lily with him, richer by ten times than the same toil would have made him back in the states. He'd have been afraid then, but the Vigilantes had broken the back of Plummer's outlaw band, and the trail had been safe. And the richest thing he'd packed they couldn't have stolen from him, anyway—an idea.

A mighty good idea, as these twenty-eight years since had proved. He might not have been the brightest man to settle in Montana Territory, but he'd noticed a thing or two at Virginia City. It wasn't the men who dug the gold who ended up rich, he'd observed. Base a future on what a claim would bring, and you likely ended up sore-backed and busted. Cattle would be the coming thing, he'd judged, and he'd got him some, once he'd hunted out land to his liking. He'd started this ranch from scratch and fought off roving Sioux and Crow and a few rustlers. He'd gambled on weather and market and ridden in heat and cold. He'd come through the Big Die of '86–'87 better than most. Maybe he'd been entitled to a little fear in the ranch-building years, too, but he'd been too busy then to think about it.

He prowled the parlor morosely, lost in himself, not liking the things on his mind, the way the years had worked out. Now you had a country all settled up, and the young whippersnappers like Duke talking law-and-order, telling you plain that the old way was past so that even when a Lark Rigby talked of tearing down your fence, you played it peaceful. And so there was fear. Not for yourself, but for Duke riding alone somewhere tonight, armed only with a six-shooter and a notion that made no sense because you had lived by a rougher code.

He sighed, reckoning that he should get on out to the bunkhouse. Maybe Duke was there, rolled in his blankets. Maybe Duke had ridden in after that girl had put out the lamp and, seeing the house dark, had supposed his old dad long gone to bed and so hadn't even looked to see if Gulley Jordan's bunk was empty or not. And that was another thing that didn't set well, he reflected, being pushed out of his own bed and his own house, along with Duke, because they'd got them a female bookkeeper and people mustn't be given anything to talk about, what with Duke's not getting around to that wedding.

He moved back to the table to blow out the lamp. Only then did he see the scrap of paper and make out the blur of writing. He looked around for his glasses and began cussing till he found them shoved back on his thatch of hair. He got them onto his nose, and the words of the note took shape:

Dad Jordan:

You fell asleep in your chair, so I am going to put out the lamp. Duke came home a little while ago, but we felt it best not to wake you. He's gone again and may not be back for a while. Please do not worry. I'm riding into Signal tonight on a little errand. It may be quite late before I get back.

Dorcas

He crumpled the note in his huge fist and flung it away. Then he kicked the blanket that lay on the floor, the one the girl had put around his legs. "Duke came home . . . we felt it best not to wake you . . ." More of the same. More of this treating him like an old horse put out to pasture. Plain as print what they were really thinking: Gulley Jordan had got too old. Too old to run his own ranch. Too old to be trusted with truths. And so they left him alone, blanket wrapped and made comfortable as could be, left him to fears that were the more dreadful because nowadays he was always left groping in the dark.

He blew out the lamp and stood for a moment, the reek of coal-oil strong. And in that moment, he knew, suddenly, why Riley Buckner's name had been wrung from him. He had remembered a man he'd known when he'd been his own man. And he had reached out in a dream for what used to be. Riley was out of jail now, they said. No matter. There was a gate between him and Ry Buckner, and he'd closed that gate himself five years ago and locked it and thrown the key away. And maybe he'd been wrong—maybe he'd been wrong. Thinking this, his loneliness turned sharper and became a curse to carry to bed.

In the shadow of a giant cottonwood a hundred yards beyond Boxed J's ranch-house, Dorcas Lane had reined up on the road toward Signal and turned in her saddle for a long look back. House and bunkhouse and barn lay formless; and lost in that same shrouding darkness and traveling his own trail in another direction would be Duke. Duke carrying food she'd hastily sacked for him. Duke riding in fear and shock. She shook her head, not wanting to think of Duke and his danger. Much might be asked of her now. Worry wouldn't make for a clear mind.

Until this moment, she realized, she'd been too busy to give full thought to what Duke had told her when he'd ridden home from one night excursion an hour ago, only to start out on another. Clear, though, was the picture of him pacing the dimly lighted kitchen, words tumbling from him as his father snored in the parlor beyond. She'd packed the food while Duke talked. She'd gone into the yard afterwards and seen him climb back to saddle and head out. He'd been so agitated he hadn't thought to kiss her. Right then she'd known precisely what she must do this very night, so she'd gone back into the house and dressed for the trail.

The note would tell Gulley Jordan all he needed to know. He hadn't found the note yet, for the house was as dark as she'd left it.

She faced forward again, flicking the reins and lifting the horse to a trot. She'd be getting into Signal mighty late as it was, considering the errand to be done. She wished the moon would get through the cloud rack above; she wished the wind were less cold. She was no child afraid of the dark, but tonight calamity had struck, casting its own kind of shadow; and she shivered in spite of herself. Who knew who rode the valley and for what reason? But that would be Duke's lookout, not hers. She had learned long ago to face realities and, if needs be, shape them to her own ambitions. Again she told herself that she must think only of her plan.

This was broken country, land of rock and bluff and stunted tree, but her horse knew the road and kept to it. Ahead a cutbank loomed. She did not see the rider in its shadow until she was almost upon him, and then she made out a tall, heavy-shouldered form sitting a saddle. The man might have been Duke himself, except that Duke was heading toward the Garnet Hills, so the name that leaped into her mind was Riley Buckner's. She almost shouted it. She knew then how close to the edge of her thinking Ry had lingered lately, ever since the news a month ago that he was out of Deer Lodge. But now the man moved his horse toward her, blocking her, and she realized he wasn't Riley. He reached out a hand and grasped her bridle.

"Miss Lane?" he asked, peering at her. "Where you going?"

She knew him now—Abe Lofstrum, one of the dozen or so Hatchet riders. He was like Duke and Ry only in build, for he was a dozen years older. Her voice tight, she said, "I'm going to town. Let me by."

"Easy, now," he said: "I got a couple of questions. Is Duke back there at the house?"

"No, he isn't."

"Seen him lately?"

"Take your hand off that bridle," she said. "I don't have to answer your questions!"

His voice hardened. "Hatchet isn't owing Boxed J any politeness tonight. You'll answer me, miss, or I'll wring it out of you. One of the two."

She brought her quirt up and lashed at his face. He shied back, releasing his hold. She struck at him again, then brought the quirt hard against the rump of her horse. The mount bolted forward. She heard Lofstrum shout at her. She galloped hard, flogging the horse again and again. She looked over her shoulder but couldn't be sure whether Lofstrum was in pursuit. She bent low over the saddlehorn and raced on, holding to this pace till the horse began to flag. She looked back again. No sign of the Hatchet rider.

She panted in relief, but she knew why he had given up the chase, and the thought troubled her. He wasn't concerned with her; he was watching for Duke. His job was to guard the road to town, to see that Duke didn't take that road; and so he hadn't risked chasing her and thus leaving the backtrail open. Well, he'd wait in vain for Duke to come this way; but the point remained that if one trail was already guarded, so, too, might be the others. How thin had Hatchet spread its crew tonight, and how swiftly?

She rode on. She had turned wary of every shadow, suspicious of every tree or rock big enough to hide a rider. She galloped the horse at intervals and begrudged the periods when she had to pull the mount back to a walk. At last she came into Signal, following the road until it became Bottom Street, the town's main thoroughfare which straggled along the V sides of the slopes.

Nearly midnight, she guessed, and only a few lights showing. The moon rode clear now, and she could see horses at the hitchrail before the Frontier Bar farther along, but she didn't continue on Bottom Street. Instead, she turned up a cross street climbing the north slope and swung from her saddle before the snug cottage of Oliver Landers, the county clerk. She lurched as she took her first step.

Nobody strolled this quiet area, and most houses were dark. From Bottom, the sounds of the Frontier lifted with startling clarity in that peculiar cupped-in way of gulches, and from the benchland topping the south slope came the chuffing of a freight engine. Light fell from Landers' parlor window upon his neat yard, and when she let herself through the gate she glimpsed the man, his small body curled in a chair, a book in his lap.

He looked astonished when he opened the door to her knock. "Why, it's Dorcas Lane," he said. "What are you doing out at this hour?"

She'd known him since her childhood; she could remember when his muttonchop whiskers had been a sandy brown instead of gray. "Oliver," she said, "I want you to go to the courthouse with me. Tonight. I want to buy a marriage license."

He chuckled, peering at her there on the porch. He was a bachelor and an incurable romantic, and in her estimation something of a fool. "You and Duke, I assume," he said. "Can't it wait till tomorrow?"

He doesn't know, she thought. *If the news has got to town, it hasn't got to him.* "Oliver, it can't wait," she said. "Please, Oliver!"

She knew she was a pretty girl; she knew this without conceit. Also, she knew how pliable almost any man might be if she coached her pleas in the right tone. She saw him hesitate, then soften. She had won. "Just a minute till I get my coat," he said. He chuckled again. "All you young folks are alike. The rest of us know months in advance that you're going to get hitched, but once you make up your own minds, you'd think the world was coming to an end the next day."

He couldn't know how close he'd come to her fear. *Maybe it is,* she thought. *Oh, God, maybe it is!*

He seemed to take forever getting his coat and hat. She curbed her impatience, needing his good will. When they left, they walked together, Dorcas leading her horse. They didn't descend to Bottom Street at once; they paralleled it on Step Street, the first one up this north slope, then struck downward when the courthouse was directly below them. A light burned in the sheriff's office adjacent to the jail section in the basement; the rest of the building lay dark. Landers led the way up the broad front steps, fumbled out his keys, and opened the ponderous door. All his movements were irritatingly slow. They groped along a hallway to his office, where he got a lamp lighted.

"Most usually a couple come together," he observed as he adjusted the wick. "But the law doesn't require it."

"I know," she said. "I looked up the law once. A license can be bought by mail, for that matter."

He glanced at her sharply. "That's right. Provided the correct information is supplied."

She nodded. "Christian and surnames of the fathers of both parties. Christian and maiden names of the mothers. Christian and surnames of the marrying parties. Residences of both, their places of birth, their ages, their colors, and whether or not either has been married before."

"That's absolutely right!" he said in admiration. He got out a form, dipped a pen in ink, and eyed her quizzically. She reeled off the information as if by rote. He seemed to take forever to write it down, but at last she held the certificate and paid him the two dollar fee. He blew out the lamp, and they groped to the big front door, which he carefully locked. She bade him good night then and thanked him.

"Are you heading right back to the ranch?" he asked.

"Yes," she said.

He shook his head. "I certainly hope no real trouble comes of that fence dispute between Gulley and Lark Rigby."

He doesn't know, she thought again. *Thank heavens the news hasn't got about!*

She went to her horse which she had tied to the courthouse fence. Landers gave her a salute and started up the sidestreet towards home. She climbed to the saddle and walked her mount along Bottom, heading west. When she drew abreast of the Frontier, the saloon's roar reached out to her. She counted five Hatchet horses at the hitchrail. She rode on past, almost not seeing Sam Tull, who stood beside the building just beyond the window. He stared at her from beneath his hat brim, saying nothing, making no move.

She knew Tull well, his relentlessness and the streak of brutality in him and the strong drive of ambition that was his constant spur. She thought of Duke then, somewhere out yonder in the lonely night. She thought of the marriage license in her name and Duke's in her pocket. She was an honest person who knew herself thoroughly, and she had long been pursued by her own kind of ambition. But in this moment she was all woman, unselfish, thinking only of her man and his danger. She said a silent prayer for Duke and rode on along the street and out of town.

3 : Man Blocked

Buckner came down the south slope walking boldly, done with skulking. He had clung to shadows when he'd first quitted the Lane house; he had kept alert for any sight or sound of the six men hunting him, but they had moved on, not guessing that he'd hidden in Pru's bedroom a while. He saw no one. He supposed there was a strong chance that Hatchet had given up the hunt. He remembered Rufe York in that back room of the Frontier saying they were wasting time and urging that they get riding. He remembered Spence Rigby's soft, "Soon, Rufe. Soon." It was Duke they really wanted tonight, for their own reasons. It was Duke they had probably gone after now.

But regardless, he had had enough of skulking. Damned if a man should play the dog dodging a kick. Thinking this, he had taken to the boardwalk on angry impulse, his shoulders thrust back and his fists doubled. He began to wish that any one of the six would show; and he wondered if he should have borrowed Pru's gun. No need. He reckoned his fists would do.

He was heading for the courthouse. The immense bulk of the building loomed before him, and he had descended nearly to Bottom Street at the corner where the courthouse stood when he saw Dorcas. She stood talking to Oliver Landers, the moonlight full on her face, and now she walked to a waiting horse and lifted herself to the saddle. She wore one of those daring new divided skirts, he saw. He looked at her, the closeness that had once been theirs strong in memory, and he stood stock still and almost called her name.

He mustn't, he knew. Not after her last letter. She had written regularly in his first two prison years, warm letters and then some that were merely kind, and finally the letter that had said they'd best forget each other. They had been too long apart, she'd claimed, and her own world had moved on. And so he watched her move away now, following her with his eyes as she rode past mercantile and post office and blacksmith shop, shuttered for the night, past the Frontier Bar, and then out of sight.

He felt numb. He had stood a chance with her once; he'd have liked to tear down whatever barrier the lost years had put between them. Then why had he stayed tongue-tied when he might have called out to her?

Chance come, chance gone. He shrugged. Then he looked at the courthouse, the windows of the three-story structure like so many dead eyes, save for the light showing in Sheriff Virgil McQueen's quarters in the basement.

Time to walk softly again. He had grown up with the constant legend of McQueen. He wondered if his notion were worth the risk he'd take breaking into the courthouse tonight. A wind roamed the street, cold with autumn's bite, pushing at him, and suddenly his plan seemed childish and futile. Yet he remembered his earlier thought—you looked for what you'd lost where you'd lost it—and hope took hold of him. He walked around the corner and climbed the low iron fence and eased into the shadows along the basement wall on the opposite side of the building from McQueen's quarters.

He had found one open window tonight when he had needed it, but the courthouse should not be so accessible, he knew. Still, he moved along the row of basement windows to a certain one and knelt and fumbled with the sash. It stuck at first, but when he exerted pressure, the sash lifted. He smiled; he had not run out of luck yet. He climbed down into the darkness of a storage room, groped across it to a door, and let himself into a corridor.

He paused, listening hard. Odd how noisy a nearly empty building could be. He edged along the corridor, attained a stairs and climbed to the next floor and then on up to the third. He moved slowly. The hall was a tunnel of darkness, but memory served him. To his left would be the district judge's chambers, to his right the county attorney's office. At the end of the hall he came against a door. He fumbled for the knob and let himself into the courtroom. Tall windows stood along the south and west walls, but the moon had moved into another cloud rack. He waited for it to show again, letting his eyes grow accustomed to the gloom meanwhile.

Gradually he made out the railing that partitioned the seats of the spectators from the judge's bench, the tables for attorneys and their clients, the jury box.

Nothing was changed. From the wall a framed portrait of a judge turned United States senator glared at him, and bracketed nearby hung a .44 caliber Henry repeater rifle that had made history and was reputed to be kept loaded. Brass cuspidors dotted the floor. Best watch that he didn't stumble over one.

He moved toward the railing, and the floor creaked beneath him. He hesitated. The west end of the courtroom was directly over McQueen's quarters, but there was one story between them. He climbed the railing and moved to one of the long tables and pulled back a chair and seated himself,

Now, he thought. *Now!*

And nothing happened.

He sat for a full minute, trying to people this room as it had been the last day he'd spent here. Again the whole business seemed futile, childish, and he wondered if prison had addled him. He remembered long-termers slack of mouth and wild of speech, and he shuddered. He put his whole concentration on what he'd hoped to learn here; and then they came, the ghosts of yesteryear.

First, Samuel Acton, his court-appointed attorney. Acton, who had slumped in the chair next to him, his ample vest stained with tobacco juice, his white mane looking churned. Acton, his whiskey breath poorly disguised by cloves, his skill discarded bit by bit with a thousand empty bottles. And now Granville Cross, the county attorney, thin and sharp as a rapier, was at the next table. And the sheriff and the other officials and the horde of spectators who had heard the verdict of two days earlier and returned to hear the sentencing.

And up there on the bench, Judge Rance, pompous and self-righteous and given to long-winded speeches.

He waited now for Rance's voice, and it came at last, so clear in recall as seeming to be speaking from the emptiness behind the bench, the voice ordering him to be brought forward. He got up from the chair, compelled by this strange re-enactment. He stood before the bench.

"Riley Buckner, you have been found guilty of grand larceny by a jury of your peers, with the nature of your punishment left to my discretion. The sentence I shall pronounce has been determined in accordance with the nature of your offense and the jury's recommendation that some leniency be shown. In my opinion, however, there is a greater offense of which you are guilty, but it is not punishable by law. I refer to the offense of ingratitude."

He stood straighter as he had that other time; he had told himself he must not flinch from the blow.

"According to the testimony, you came among us as a boy of five in 1870. You were brought here by your father, a professional gambler, who died five years later in a shooting affray involving an accusation that he cheated. That you seem never to have known your mother and therefore had none of the softening influence that her love might have brought you is regrettable. That you were orphaned at the age of ten is equally regrettable. It appears that thereafter you were a ward of the town, splitting wood and performing other chores for a meal or a night's lodging from your tenth year to your eighteenth. During that period, you were a boyhood friend of Duke Jordan, who eventually persuaded his father to hire you as a rider on his Boxed J ranch.

"Whether you were a favored employee because of your close friendship with the owner's son is beside the point. The fact remains that you were trusted—and you betrayed that trust. The evidence is irrefutable. I shall repeat it briefly so that you may understand why I feel that the sentence I shall pass is lenient indeed.

"One month ago you and Duke Jordan and other Boxed J riders were sent to deliver a herd of cattle over the mountains to Jupiter City. Once delivery was made and the cattle sold, the other riders returned to the home ranch. You and Duke Jordan, however, remained in Jupiter for several days and were seen roistering in various saloons and gambling establishments. Duke agrees that you urged that both of you return home, and he further testifies that he sent you on with a carpetbag containing the herd money while he tarried among the fleshpots.

"You have claimed that at a specified point on the trail you were attacked at a night camp by a masked rider, and the bag containing the money was stolen. You told of a futile search over several days for the unknown bandit. Finally you returned to Boxed J to find that Duke had reached home meanwhile. Your story of the robbery might have been believed, except that two hundred dollars of the missing money was found under the ticking of your bunk. That money has been identified by serial number as having been issued by the Jupiter City bank to the purchaser of the cattle.

"Your attorney has made every possible effort on your behalf. He has hinted at a frame-up. By whom or for what reason, he could not even guess. Therefore the evidence seems conclusive that, in the eyes of the law, you are guilty of grand larceny. In the eyes of humanity, you are also guilty, as I have said, of ingratitude.

"Consider: You were a homeless waif given a position of trust by Gulley Jordan because of the friendship of his son. You betrayed that trust by stealing from your employer.

"Now it remains my duty to pass sentence. The statutes of the Territory of Montana establish the penalty for your crime at not less than one nor more than fourteen years in prison. I now relegate you to the custody of the sheriff until such time as he can deliver your person to Deer Lodge penitentiary where you are to serve five years of confinement at whatever labor the warden shall allot you. Have you any legal cause to show why this judgment should not be pronounced against you?"

Here in the empty darkness he heard himself whisper, "I've nothing to say, Judge. Not to you, anyway."

He turned away from the bench as he'd turned that other time. He came with a ghostly McQueen beside him into the section where the spectators sat. He peered at emptiness for the white, strained face of Dorcas Lane, the hard, uncompromising stare of Gulley Jordan, the weak, handsome face of Duke. He came to where Duke had been sitting; and he paused, his own words clear in memory. "It's crossed my mind, Duke, that that jigger with the mask had just about your build."

He had waited for Duke to protest, to point out that

a score of men in Ruby County were of their same build, but Duke had only flushed, not meeting his eye. And so he had turned away from Duke and walked from this room, the law at his elbow. And now, these five years later, he had come back. But he had settled nothing by coming here, except that one thing stood clear. There was a thing sadder than the death of a friend, and that was the death of a friendship. He had been close to no man save Duke. The only thing left was to see Duke.

That was it. There was no answer to be found in empty darkness. He had to face Duke and put a question to him, and the real question was not whether Duke had framed him and so killed what had been between them, but *why?*

He'd get some sleep first, and then he would rent a horse at Jake Hollis's livery stable and hit the trail for Boxed J. He would find Duke and settle this matter forever. After that, he would pick up the broken thread of his life again. He turned toward the door and then he stopped, chilled by the certainty that someone else was here. No ghost harked up from memory but someone real. He tried to see into the deeper darkness beyond the open doorway. He called softly, "Who's there?"

From the hall, Virgil McQueen said, "Put your hands up. That's right." McQueen came forward and Buckner could make him out now, tall and angular and implacable of face, standing there in his stocking feet, a six-shooter held level in his right hand.

"Buckner, eh?" McQueen said. "You're late getting

back to us. About thirty days late. You see, they send me word when they turn one of you loose."

"And you let the word get around, McQueen. But you've got no reason to be holding a gun on me now."

McQueen sighed. "This building has been busier than a camp meeting tonight. Heard a couple people come in a while ago, but they used a key at the front door. That made their business honest. Then somebody started prowling. I figured I'd better have a look."

"No law against standing in an empty courtroom, McQueen."

"Depends on how you got in here."

"Breaking and entering, you think?"

"Shapes up that way."

Buckner shook his head. "The Halloween I was thirteen, Duke Jordan and I found a basement window with a broken latch. We didn't have the nerve to come inside and do mischief. Not with you living in the building. I made a bet with myself tonight that if that latch wasn't found and fixed then, it would still be broken these fourteen years later. I was right."

McQueen said, "So you didn't break in. Then the question comes down to this: what were you after?"

"You won't swallow the answer. I just wanted to stand where I'd stood once before. I wanted to straighten out my thinking."

"About Duke?"

Buckner started. "How would you know that?"

"I remember what you said to him when I walked you out of here. I was close enough to hear."

"Then you can guess what's bothering me."

"The suspicion that Duke took that money bag from you? And then planted some of the cash in your bunk to make a case against you?"

"That's pretty nearly the size of it, McQueen. You letting me walk out of here?"

"To hunt down Duke?"

"I've got a question to ask him."

McQueen held silent for a long moment. "A few others will be hunting Duke, too. There'll be me, with a badge. There'll be Spence Rigby with a lynch rope and a bad case of hangtree fever. There'll be Sam Tull with his own dark notions, and maybe a few other folks. Duke will likely be moving too fast to answer any questions."

Alarm touched Buckner. "Duke running? Hatchet was watching for him at the depot tonight. McQueen, what the hell's happened on this range since I left?"

"What's happened happened tonight. Sam Tull brought the word to me from Hatchet about ten o'clock. Duke Jordan took a ride early this evening. He found Lark Rigby and Sam cutting a fence Boxed J put up along the Strip. Hot words got said. And Duke shot Lark Rigby dead. You savvy how that shapes up?"

Yes, he savvied. Much that had made no sense earlier tonight was now understandable, but the truth stunned him. Duke a hunted killer, with the law and the lawless on his trail! Duke running, and his own scheme blocked now because Duke would be making himself hard to find. Five prison years of uncertainty he'd known—five years of weighing what Duke had once meant to him against the suspicion he had about Duke.

He thought, *God help you, Duke!* and that was the old friendship crying out. His second thought was that he still had to get to Duke, regardless. The difference now was that he had to reach him first.

4 : The Violent Ones

He heard McQueen's voice as from afar. "Reckon you're hard hit, boy. Follows you would be. What you need is a cup of coffee and maybe a bait of grub. How does that sound?"

This astonished Buckner. He was still shaken by the news about Duke, and in any tallying of the obstacles that lay between him and reaching Duke, the presence of Virgil McQueen made the first obstacle. McQueen hadn't yet told him he was free to walk out of here. And McQueen hadn't come at him in a friendly way, not with gun in hand and a question about breaking and entering. But McQueen had turned friendly now.

"We could talk a bit," McQueen added. "Maybe we both want the same thing. Maybe we could work together getting it."

"Duke in jail, you mean?"

"I'm the law, boy. I've been the law a long time. How about that coffee?"

He knew McQueen meant it. No man for joshing,

McQueen. Buckner shrugged. "You pour it, Sheriff. I'll drink it."

"Come along," McQueen said and moved down the hall so silently that Buckner's boots sounded thunderous following him.

They dropped down the stairs to the basement where the door of McQueen's quarters now stood open, letting lamplight into the hall along which Buckner had earlier groped after coming through that storage room window. McQueen lived in a single room adjacent to his office, a room with a cot, a kitchen range propped up with bricks where one leg was missing, a lumpy sofa, an unpainted table, a few chairs. Calendars covered one wall, fly specked and time faded and overlapping each other, the milestones of the many years McQueen had been sheriff. Buckner looked at McQueen's litter, old newspapers, old mail order catalogs, old livestock journals. What this place needed was a good fire.

McQueen's boots, discarded when he'd gone catfooting upstairs, stood just inside the door. He stomped into them, walked over to the stove and pulled the coffee pot to a front lid. He motioned his guest to a chair. Buckner took one by the table. From where he sat, he could see through another open doorway into the office beyond, where a second lamp burned. McQueen poked into a cupboard, getting tin cups.

Buckner was having his first real look at the sheriff, and he saw that McQueen had aged. The same tall, angular frame, yes, but the shoulders were stooped. The same weathered, implacable face, but flabby somehow, not so strong. McQueen must be pushing seventy. He'd been—let's see—sheriff since about '75, and a

Kansas trail-town peace officer before that, holding the lid down in places like Caldwell and Wichita and Dodge City, carving out a reputation that still stood alongside the legends of Earp and Masterson and Hickok. And before that, or so it was told, a Civil War infantryman, wearing the blue of some Michigan volunteer regiment. Yes, the man added up to a lot of years and a lot of tales, but even a rock wore with time.

McQueen fetched the pot from the stove, clanked down the cups on the table, and poured the coffee. It smelled mighty good. McQueen took his own cup in both hands and blew the steam away. "A man deals with people, he gets so he can call the shot on them every time," he said reflectively. "The only way they ever fool you is by turning out more decent than you thought. Reckon Spence Rigby won't shape up that way, though. I'm betting I'm going to have callers any time now. Hatchet wanting my official blessing to hide behind when they do a lynching."

Buckner shook his head. "Lark and Spence hating each other all these years, and now Spence ramrods Hatchet!"

"Sole survivor, so sole heir, boy. Unless there was a will stating otherwise, and there isn't. I asked Sam Tull about that tonight." He took a sip of the coffee. "I'll not spar with you in the time that's left, Ry. You want Duke, and so do I. How would you like to wear a deputy badge?"

He looked at McQueen and was beyond surprise. Then he laughed. "Jailbird a month ago. Right-hand of the law a month later. That would be coming up in the world." He shook his head again. "You're probably the one sheriff in Montana who never appointed a deputy. I've heard tell you keep a drawer full of badges and never have passed one out. You used to say you didn't want anybody in your way when trouble started. Why the change, McQueen?"

McQueen sighed. "You grew up with Duke, boy. You were as close to him as paper to the wall. You know how he'd think, where he'd head. You could gain two jumps on him to my one."

"And fetch him back for a legal hanging?"

"Maybe. That would be for the court to decide. Our job would only be to bring him in."

"But I didn't say I wanted to bring him in. I just want to straighten out my thinking about him."

"You've had five years for that, Ry. So have I. One of three things happened. Some galoot with a mask—call him Rider X—took that money bag from you; but if so, why did he bother planting currency in your bunk to put you in stony lonesome? A straight-out robber wouldn't have had a personal grudge, likely. Possibility two: you stole that money yourself, just as the court believed, and made the mistake of leaving some of it where it was found. Number three: Duke was Rider X and then planted evidence against you for reasons we don't know about. That was the notion biting at you when you made your remark to him on the way out of court. I've turned the whole thing over in my mind a heap of times. I've come to that notion myself."

"But you could be wrong."

McQueen's voice took on an edge sharp as the wind that roamed beyond these walls. "I'm offering you a badge. I won't offer it again."

Buckner took a swig of his coffee, needing to think. Wear a badge, and he could hunt down Duke and still ask the question he had to put to Duke. The difference was that, regardless, as a lawman he'd still have to bring Duke in. Thinking this, he saw the badge as one more obstacle. He had to ride as his own man. He put down the coffee cup. "I reckon not, McQueen."

McQueen said in that same sharp voice, "Better a badge than the bars in yonder jail section, boy."

Buckner stiffened. "Meaning—?"

"So you didn't break and enter, since the window had a busted lock. Just the same, it could go on the books as illegal entry. There's money in the county treasurer's office and a bit scattered here and there in other places. How would a court see the situation? A man has been convicted once of larceny. He comes back from prison, and if you shook him by the heels right now, I'm betting, you'd strew mighty little silver on the floor. So he's found prowling the courthouse, maybe trying the door of the treasurer's office. You see how it would stack up?"

Buckner rose from the chair. "McQueen, I grew up on talk of you," he said hotly. "I've heard tell you have a badge where your heart ought to be. I've heard you'd follow a man to the gates of hell if the law had a claim on him. I've heard a lot of things tallying up to your being the toughest lawman this side of Texas. But I never heard tell that you played any game the crooked way. You know damn' well what brought me into this building tonight!"

McQueen said stonily, "Just the same, I've given you a choice, boy."

Buckner stared at him, stared at a legend shattered. McQueen had that implacable look, but a red flush marked the taut skin across his cheekbones. Anger or shame? Buckner didn't know; he only knew he would not submit to the implied blackmail. He kept staring at McQueen, hot words storming through his mind. He sorted out the words, wanting the sharpest ones to fling at McQueen, but he didn't get them said. Someone was laying a heavy fist against the street door leading into the office area beyond, and that was Spence Rigby's voice shouting, "Sheriff! Open up! We want to talk to you!"

Buckner remembered now that McQueen had guessed that Hatchet would come calling soon, and Hatchet had indeed come, the sounds of approach muffled by wind and wall.

Over his shoulder, McQueen shouted, "Just a minute, Spence!" He looked across the table at Buckner, and then he did an unexpected thing. He unbuckled his gunbelt and laid it on the table between them. "I'll be through with them shortly, boy," he said. "You just wait here and think over what I offered you. Hell, Ry, I was only trying to do you a favor and me a favor at the same time."

"And if I pick up your gun and have it lined on you when you come back—?"

"Then I won't need any made-up story about you tinkering with the treasurer's door, boy. I'll really have you where the skin pinches."

Rigby's fist hammered the outer door again. "Sheriff! Open up, I say!"

McQueen turned and walked into the office area.

Buckner knew that room, more littered than this one, a cubbyhole dominated by a big rolltop pigeonhole desk stuffed with papers. McQueen passed from his sight, but he could hear the sheriff unbolt and wrench open the street door. The lamp out there flared wildly to a gust of wind, and Rigby's voice came loud. "What the hell kept you, Virg? Asleep?"

McQueen said evenly, "It's that time of night, Spence."

Rigby's voice turned shrill with anger. "You pound your ear while a killer rides loose? Must be three hours now since Sam Tull brought you the news. Most of Hatchet has ridden in, gathering at my place. They make up a posse. I've been telling them you'd show any minute to lead us. And all this time you've been sleeping!"

McQueen said stiffly, "I don't need you to tell me how to handle my job, Spence. I've been a manhunter a long time. I never gained anything ramming around in the middle of a night, lighting matches in the windy dark to look for sign. Duke's trail will be easier cut come daylight."

"Virg, are you saying you don't intend to ride tonight?"

"I'll bring him in, Spence. In my own time and in my own way."

"We don't plan to wait on that, Virg. We're riding tonight. Will you swear us in as deputies?"

"No," McQueen said flatly. "I won't."

Buckner moved forward then, compelled by a sense that the clash in the next room had come to crisis. As he moved, he plucked McQueen's six-shooter from its holster, then bent and blew out the lamp so there would be no light behind him. He got to the doorway between the two rooms and stood there. He could now see McQueen's stiffened back, and beyond McQueen, Rigby, his round face ablaze with anger, and beyond Rigby a shapeless mass of mounted men out there in the street, those violent ones, dark and silent. That high form to the fore would be Sam Tull.

Rigby said, "Then it stacks up to this, Virg: You won't do your job, and you won't empower us to do it for you. Is that right?"

McQueen said, "Listen to me, Spence. For all his faults, Lark Rigby stood for something hereabouts, and he was as much a friend of mine as any man. You're his inheritor, it seems, but that doesn't change the fact that Lark had no use for you and that you smarted because everybody knew it. So now you're hell-bent on squaring for Lark. Why, Spence? Could it be you've got hangtree fever because, one, you've never stacked very high in anybody's eyes and here's your chance to get even with the whole world, and two, by getting Lark's killer you'll be pretending that Lark meant something to you, which will make Lark look wrong for not having given a hoot for you? Either case, you don't aim to bring Duke in. You aim to run him down and lynch him."

Rigby's face got redder. "Man, I'm asking to be deputized! I'm even asking that you come along! How do you make hangtree fever out of that?"

"You're asking to have the law with you or the sanction of the law or both. That would help clear your skirts afterwards. You want it to look like you rode out law-abiding. Too bad that once we caught Duke, you and your bunch threw a gun on the sheriff, being over-come by grief and anger when you laid eyes on the killer. You hadn't started out with any lynching notion, you'll say; otherwise you'd never have brought the sher-iff along or got deputized in the first place. But I know you, Spence, and I read the scheme that's in you."

Rigby said in a convulsed voice, "Virg, damn you—!"

"I'm not finished," McQueen said. "Look at that pack behind you. Hatchet hands who remember that Lark was a pretty decent boss. Men easy twisted when the time comes. And Sam Tull heading them. A bigger brute than you, Spence. A man who worked for Lark but *hated* him every minute because Lark was the boss and he was the hired hand. And this is the outfit you want deputized! Now get out of here! Have the decency to bury your dead before you do anything else. You forgot how it might look to folks if Lark's funeral doesn't come first?"

That last gave Rigby pause. Buckner could see the man start. But Rigby's bluster came back. "We'll take care of Lark. But we'll be riding afterwards."

"Not with any blessing of mine, Spence."

From behind Rigby, Sam Tull's voice came, flat and cold. "Don't stand arguing with him, Spence. He's got too old for his job. A lot of us have known that for a long time, and the next election will wash him out. Walk in there and help yourself to some badges. We'll tell the town we asked him to do his duty and he wouldn't."

McQueen fell back a pace. "Don't try it!" he said. "I'm warning you!"

He'd made a mistake, taking that one backward step, Buckner knew. The second mistake was that McQueen had let his voice break. Until this moment he had been implacable and magnificent, holding back Hatchet by sheer force of nerve, that and the legend behind him. But Rigby moved a step forward now, a knowledge of victory naked in his eyes. Until Buckner spoke.

"Far enough, Spence," he said and moved from the doorway on into the office, McQueen's gun held level.

"Buckner," Rigby said and drew in a deep breath. His eyes squinted tighter, and he almost looked asleep. "We should have kept hunting you, I see, instead of turning back for more important business. We should have run you down and stomped you into the ground."

"Lost chance," Buckner said. "I've got a gun now."

From the rim of the lamplight spilling through the street doorway, Tull's voice lifted. "There's near a dozen of us out here, Buckner. Throw that gun down."

Buckner shook his head. "You've got the odds, granted. But the first one to die will be Spence. Then, if I've another second left, I'll try for you, Sam."

McQueen's face showed nothing, but he'd moved to one side, clearing the space between Buckner and the street doorway. Rigby stood hesitant. He'd pulled a slicker over his black gambler's garb as a windbreaker, and he looked like a huge, yellow grizzly with a round, bloated face. His mouth had gone slack. He said in a harsh whisper, "Easy, Sam! Don't start anything!"

His eyes locked with Buckner's and held hard for a full five seconds. Then Rigby broke. He backed to the door. "Another time, another place, Ry," he said and backed on out and pulled the door shut behind him.

McQueen stepped over and slid the bolt. He looked at Buckner. In the lamplight sweat glistened on Mc-

Queen's forehead. Without a word, Buckner turned and walked back into the other room. McQueen followed him. Buckner slid the six-shooter into the holster on the table. He took a match from his pocket and lighted the lamp, then faced McQueen. "You'll mind that I didn't line the gun on you."

McQueen said, "They'll still ride after Duke. The only difference is they can't pretend they're doing it in the law's name. I tried to stop them. You must have heard what was said."

"They'll ride," Buckner agreed. "They were looking over a county map earlier tonight, planning how to spread their net, I suppose. Your mistake was facing them unarmed."

But saying this, he suddenly realized that McQueen had planned it so. The gun hadn't been left behind as some sort of temptation for Riley Buckner. Nor had McQueen counted on his coming to the rescue. McQueen had shucked his gun to be sure he'd have no call to use it. And now Buckner remembered Tull's "He's got too old for his job," and he remembered, too, McQueen's trying to blackmail him into taking a deputy's badge. McQueen had been that desperate for help. Truly, time had worn away the rock.

"There was unfinished business between us when they came," he reminded McQueen.

McQueen sat down, his shoulders slumping. "Get out of here, boy," he said.

"I'm free to walk out?"

McQueen looked up at him, and he saw the suffering in the sheriff's eyes. "You said you'd never heard tell of my playing any game the crooked way. But you know I tried to hold a club over you tonight. Maybe in the years to come, there'll be a time when you'll understand why. And when you do, just remember something else: I didn't repay a favor with a disfavor. Now get out of here!"

"I'll be taking Duke's trail, too, McQueen."

"Of course," McQueen said. The old implacable look stiffened his face again. "You want to believe in Duke because he was that close to you that believing in him is believing in yourself. You want him to tell you he didn't frame you five years ago, and maybe he didn't. Comes the showdown, you may even be on his side. So be it. But you go standing against the law, and I'll bring you in right along with him. Just keep that in mind."

"I'll remember," Buckner said. He walked into the office then and slipped back the bolt on the door and stepped out into the empty, wind-swept street.

5 : **Gulley Loads a Gun**

Dorcas lifted her neglected coffee cup and found it cold. Here in the kitchen of the Boxed J ranch-house, midmorning sunlight touched the red-and-white checkered tablecloth where her breakfast had been spread, and across from her Gulley Jordan sat. She had finished her say to him, and it had taken a lot of talking. She'd tried not to look at him the while. She had slept late and breakfasted late, and he had come in and found her eating here alone, and she had asked him to sit. He had done so grudgingly. He didn't much like her, she knew. But he had sat, and he'd listened, and she had told him nearly all of it, how Duke had come in last night with his wild talk of having shot a man and how she had packed food for him and he had headed out, a fugitive.

She had known that the old man would have to be told. She'd faced that fact on the ride home from Signal, coming through the night wary and watchful but finding Abe Lofstrum gone from his post beneath the cutbank. She had fallen into bed exhausted. She had awakened hoping that daylight would dispel the horror of the night, but it hadn't. She had made her breakfast and heard the old man bang through the back door. No easy task it had been to tell him his son was a killer, wanted by the law and hunted by Hatchet, too.

And now he sat in the same tight-lipped silence in which he had listened, an ancient lump of a man. His thin white hair seemed no more than the ghost of hair; and it struck her that his face, which ran mostly to beak, might have been hewn from granite. He must be terribly hard hit, and she felt sorry for him and wanted to reach across the table and touch his hand. She didn't dare. At best he only tolerated her, and his resentment, she guessed, was because of Duke. He hadn't wanted to share Duke with anyone, but twice he'd had to. There had been Riley Buckner before that sorry business five years ago, and now there was herself.

He looked up at her. He would ask, she supposed, what had taken her into town in the dead of night. And she would have to tell him about the marriage license, for the talk would be around soon anyway, what with Oliver Landers to spread it. But she saw no question in the old man's eyes but something else instead, some secret knowledge; and suddenly she was aghast, realizing that he was inwardly laughing at her, a harsh laughter without humor.

"Been talking to Billy Larb," he said. "You'll recollect he rides into town on Wednesday nights for prayer meeting and sometimes stays over. He got back early this morning."

Billy Larb, that Boxed J hand with a religious streak! She'd forgotten about Billy and his weekly trip to town. And now this old man was telling her he'd already got the news, and his harsh laughter lay in having made a fool of her by letting her tell him what he already knew. Anger flared in her. "You might have said so at the beginning!" she snapped.

"Just wanted to maybe pick up a few more pieces to fit into the thing. According to Billy, town talk this morning has it that Spence Rigby rods Hatchet now, being Lark's only kin. Sam Tull strings along with that. And Hatchet is out for blood. Virg McQueen started after Duke at sun-up, riding alone. Now just where did Duke head? I figure he told you, girl."

"The Garnet Hills," she said. She might have been more explicit, but she was still angry.

"A big hunk of country," he said wryly.

"He shouldn't have run, probably. I tried at first to talk him out of it, but he claimed he wouldn't stand a chance otherwise."

"Depends. A gun fight wasn't necessarily murder in my day, girl."

"He got to the Strip fence last night, and Lark was there, and Sam Tull. Lark was using a pair of wire cutters. Duke threw a gun on him and told him to quit. Lark got mouthy, and Duke lost his temper. Lark started for his gun, and Duke fired then. Got Lark square between the eyes, he thinks. And Lark went down with his gun still in leather. In any case, the only witness was Tull. What kind of chance would that give Duke in a courtroom?"

"Best he ran," Gulley said. "To stew a wolf, they got to catch him first." He looked at her again, with the look one poker player gives another. "There's more news Billy fetched. Ry Buckner must have hit town last night. Billy didn't see him, but Jake Hollis said that Ry was sleeping in the haymow of his livery stable. What do you make of that?"

Ry back! Her first thought was that Gulley Jordan was giving her more news than he'd got from her; her second reaction was one of misgiving. How would Ry stand? Yesterday at this same hour the news would have set her wondering about Ry and herself and what had once been between them. Today the question was: What of Ry and Duke?

"I don't know," she said. "It depends on what fetched Ry back here."

"The money, maybe. He wouldn't tell where he hid the rest of what was in that carpetbag. Buried it in the hills, I'm thinkin', and only brought along the couple hundred that turned up in his bunk."

"Nonsense!" she said. "You don't really believe that. Anyway, if he buried currency five years ago, it would likely be ruined by now."

"Regardless, was I Ry, I'd be no friend to Boxed J, not after what happened in court. That's the point I'm considerin'. Was I Ry, I reckon I'd be pullin' for either Virg McQueen or Hatchet to catch up with Duke."

"You're not Ry," she said tartly and was instantly sorry.

"No," he said reflectively, "I'm not."

He stood up. There had still been no mention of the marriage license, and she guessed Billy Larb hadn't heard about it. Probably Billy had left town before Oliver Landers had got down to his office, from which the news would run through the courthouse and then through the town. Let Gulley Jordan learn it from the spreading gossip later. All the more reason why she must push forward quickly with her plan. She looked up. "I'll be gone again today. I thought I'd better tell you that."

He had started toward the parlor. He paused in the kitchen doorway, and it struck her now that he had changed since yesterday, grown taller, grown younger. But how could that be? She had dreaded speaking of the trouble for fear he would be crushed by the weight of it, and instead he was stronger. She even sensed a difference in his voice.

"I reckon, girl, that you know exactly where Duke has headed," he was saying. "I likewise reckon that you don't aim to tell me. But you'll be seeing him, maybe today. Just pass this word on for me. Tell him his old dad has quit sittin' in his rocking chair. Tell him anybody that gets at Gulley Jordan's cub will have to get past the old man first. He'll know then who he can count on straight across the board."

He moved on. She arose, tempted mightily to call after him, to bring him back and tell him everything, so that whatever was done, they would be pulling together instead of against each other the way they were. But she couldn't. They had in common the desire to see Duke safe, but she had her own plan to carry through, and she could guess how Gulley Jordan would interpret that. Tell him she might be marrying Duke before this day was done, and the harsh, silent laughter would show in the old man's eyes, and she would know what he thought.

No, she couldn't speak, and she must be about her own plan at once.

She picked the dishes from the table and stacked them but didn't take time to wash them. She wrote a note on a pad she kept in the kitchen, wording it very carefully, very urgently. Then she went out into the yard, into the golden morning. Around her lay the scattered buildings of Boxed J, sturdy and weathered, this man-ranch she had invaded. To the southwest the Garnet Hills lifted, Table Mountain shouldering above them all, and she looked to the hills and spoke to Duke in her heart. She started resolutely across the yard. The crew was out on the range, gone long before Billy Larb had come home with his news, but Billy himself was here, repairing a corral.

He was wrestling a peeled pole into place. He was one of those men of indefinite age; he might have been thirty—or fifty. He was reed thin and almost chinless and shy of women, and the deep religious streak in him manifested itself in more than lip service. He did not swear, he did not use tobacco or whiskey, and he had never been known to fire a gun in anger. He put down the pole as she approached, touched the brim of his hat, and to her greeting gulped and nodded.

"Billy," she asked, "how was the prayer meeting?"

"Well-attended," he said. "Your maw was there."

"Reverend Hay led you?"

"He's in Jupiter City, so it was a lay meeting. He won't be back till meeting after next."

"Billy," she said, "there was an old man through here with a wagon six or seven days ago. He was painting Scripture verses on rocks. I saw you talking to him."

He nodded. "A Campbellite, which was my father's faith."

"But is he an ordained minister?"

"The Reverend Gideon Jones, miss. A fine, sincere man."

"And that boy traveling with him?"

"His son."

She thought a moment. "Billy, I want you to saddle up for me. And I want you to saddle for yourself. I've a couple of errands for you to do."

He looked at the peeled pole at his feet; he looked toward the house where Gulley Jordan had gone.

"It's all right," she said impatiently. "Dad Jordan won't mind." She took the note she'd written and handed it to him. "Get this to my sister Pru. She'll probably be at the store helping Mother. Then ride the valley and see if you can find this Reverend Jones and his boy. You know where the old Brewster place is?"

He nodded again. "That fallen-down house in the foothills." He looked toward the Garnets. "On the old road to the Bellafonte mine. There's a cave up above Brewsters'. Duke and Riley Buckner played there when they were kids. I recollect a time Gulley sent me after them. On the way back from the cave, we got caught in a rainstorm and holed up at Brewsters'."

Her mouth went dry. The cave! How many other people knew about the cave and might remember it had once been a favorite place of Duke's? She mustn't let her fear show. "That's the place all right," she said. "Once you find Reverend Jones, ask him to head to Brewsters' and wait. I'll meet him there. Probably today, if you find him that soon."

He looked troubled. "I do not care for conspiracies, Miss."

"But you do care about Duke Jordan?"

He thought about this. "He has blood on his hands now. But it is not for me to judge. 'Vengeance is mine; I will repay, saith the Lord.' A thing for those who will be hunting Duke to remember. Those who pursue may become the hard pursued. I will do as you say."

"Good," she said. "I've a few things to gather in the bunkhouse while you're saddling."

He moved toward the barn. She stopped him. "I know you fetched the news to Dad Jordan this morning, Billy. I'm sorry you had that chore to do. It must have been very hard on him."

A great wonder spread over his guileless face. "A strange thing," he said. "I was afraid it might kill him, hearing about Duke. Instead, it was as though I had handed him a priceless treasure. The Lord works in mysterious ways, Miss."

"True," she said; yet thinking of Gulley Jordan and the change that had come over him, she was troubled. She turned toward the bunkhouse.

In the parlor, Gulley had moved straight to the object he sought, his holstered Colt Single Action revolver and belt, which hung from a hatrack made of elkhorns near the front door. He hadn't worn the old forty-five much lately. This wasn't snake country, not at this altitude, and it hadn't been wolf country in recent years, what with strychnine and bullet having cleaned them out. Got so a man wore a gun mostly for show or out of habit. Duke had argued that the Jordans best go unarmed as a safeguard against temper, considering how touchy the situation with Lark Rigby had got. And then

Duke had gone against his own advice, toting a six-shooter last night and using it and turning the calendar back twenty years, seemed like.

What a wallop Billy Larb's news had been! And the facts that girl had added to the story hadn't made it easier, indicating as they did that Duke couldn't put up the excuse of self-defense. Still, it had been worth the listening just to see her face once she'd found out he already knew about Duke. He'd let her know the old man couldn't be counted out, not yet. Damned if he hadn't.

And now there was work to be done. That was where the good lay—good come out of tragedy. Gave a man a lift, just knowing he was needed; and Duke was going to need him bad. Gave him a lift, too, knowing that for all Duke's talk about playing it peaceful, when the real cards had been dealt, Duke had done exactly what his old man would have done. Cut from the good cloth of Gullison T. Jordan, young Duke was, and that thought took away the curse of loneliness. Duke and Gulley now—against the whole blasted world, if needs be.

Duke up there in the hills somewhere. That girl knew exactly where Duke was hiding, but she wasn't saying. Never mind. It didn't matter so much where Duke was; the important thing would be to keep those hunting Duke from finding the place.

No sense standing here wasting time with all these notions running around in his head. He lifted the Colt out of leather, liking the feel of the worn walnut grip. Seventeen bucks worth of good gun. He carried the weapon to the bedroom that had been his before he'd got ousted from his own house. Here he found wiping rag and oil, and he seated himself and began cleaning the Colt. He worked slowly, carefully, having first flicked open the loading gate and punched out the six shells, one by one. And in the midst of the cleaning, he thought of Lark Rigby dead.

He had been too concerned with Duke to think about Lark before. Lark had asked for trouble and found it, a heap of it. Lark had been Boxed J's enemy, but Lark was dead now, and damned if something hadn't gone from his own life. He pondered this, scowling. And only now did he see that Lark and he were alike, even though Lark had been twenty years younger; for if it had been Lark who had put up a fence against Boxed J, it would have been Gulley Jordan who'd have come at it with wire cutters.

Never mind. Lark was dead, and a man had to concern himself with the living, and right now there was a gun to be loaded.

One of the six shells on the bed beside him was an empty, to be kept under the hammer according to custom. He picked up the first of the loaded shells and thought of those who might be hunting Duke. He slipped that first shell back into the cylinder. That one would be for Spence Rigby, who bore Lark's name but was no such man as Lark had been. A second for Sam Tull, who'd always lived by violence. He held the third shell reflectively, thinking of Virgil McQueen, who was a good man and the law. But what did an old wolf do when his cub was cornered? Let McQueen look out for himself.

The fourth shell he held for a long time. Riley Buckner? Who knew how Ry would figure in this game? But if Ry sided against Duke, then Ry had to be reckoned with. That left a fifth and last loaded shell. What name to go with the bullet? He harked up the Hatchet crew, man by man, but they were only hired hands, loyal to their salt. There would be nothing personal in any hunt they'd make for Duke.

Some sound from the yard caught his ear. He stood up, still holding that fifth shell, and walked to a window. Beyond lay the yard, and riding across it, heading out somewhere, was the girl. Going to Duke, he guessed. Well, she was one person who was on Duke's side. But could he be sure about that? He scowled again; he had never been able to name a reason for disliking Dorcas Lane, but still the feeling persisted. That girl would bear watching. And girl or no, if she turned against Duke, she became an enemy.

He went back and seated himself on the bed again. He slipped the fifth shell into the Colt and put the empty into the last chamber. He closed the loading gate and held the gun poised in his hand, ready now for anything.

6 : To the Hills

Near noon, Buckner judged, coming awake and seeing
the slant of the sunlight through the holes where shakes
had gone from the roof of Jake Hollis's livery stable.
Mighty late when he'd bedded here in the hayloft, and
mighty tired he'd been. He should be up and doing
now, but he took his time. He had learned patience in
prison; he had learned how to make haste slowly while
the endless days dwindled away.

This morning he felt eager, alive to the world. He
liked awakening with a definite purpose. In prison his
day's doings had been decided for him. When the gate
had opened, he'd known that he first had to find a job,
to make a small stake before he took his next step. Any
job would do, and he'd wrestled beer kegs at the Kess-
ler Brewery in Helena for thirty days. Then he'd started
for Signal.

He got up now and carefully brushed the straw from
his clothes. He found his boots and pulled them on.
Then he went down the loft ladder to the stall section
below. He peered into the cubby-hole that was Jake

Hollis's living quarters and found the man gone. Jake's razor lay atop a packing case that served as a bureau. He helped himself to the razor, got a bucket of water, worked up a lather from a cake of yellow soap, also Jake's, and gave himself a cold shave.

His mind was busy the while, sorting out the doings of last night. A question nearly lost in the welter of events now began pricking his curiosity. What had Dorcas been doing at the courthouse with Oliver Landers? When he'd first seen the two, he'd supposed they had met by chance and fallen to talking. But later Virgil McQueen had said that a couple of people had entered the building, using a key, which meant that one had been an official. Landers, with Dorcas? And what about Pru's hesitancy, earlier, when he'd asked about Dorcas? "Let's just say she isn't here," Pru had said. What had Pru been trying to hide?

He shrugged. Guessing got a man nowhere. But he wished more than ever that he had called out to Dorcas.

His shaving finished, he walked through the big open doorway of the livery stable and stood on Bottom Street. He saw a grim cavalcade come winding in from the west. First there was a flatbed wagon, and the man tooling it he recognized as Abe Lofstrum, Hatchet hand. Abe had a red welt across his face. On the wagon box a rough coffin rested, and behind the wagon Hatchet rode, two by two, led by Spence Rigby and Sam Tull.

Buckner took off his hat, and that was for Lark Rigby only. He had never had anything personal against Lark. Spence Rigby, looking properly mournful, kept his eyes straight ahead. So did Big Rufe York and Heck Lund and the Darbys and the other half dozen riders. Only Tull looked Buckner's way. Tull turned his death's-head of a face toward the livery; his eyes blazed, and thus he made a threat and a promise. Then the group was beyond, heading along Bottom to climb the north slope to the cemetery at its crest.

Buckner watched them go. Spence Rigby, wanting a good face on things, had taken McQueen's advice all right and gone to bury his dead, but he was wasting no time about it. Hadn't even waited for a coroner's inquest, it seemed. But at least Hatchet had been pulled this long from Duke Jordan's trail. McQueen was probably already riding.

Across the street was a restaurant. Buckner squared his shoulders and headed over. Here would be a test, but he was greeted as any man might be after five years' absence. If the few customers at this hour showed restraint, at least they showed no antagonism. It had been thus when he'd aroused Jake Hollis late last night and asked to sleep in the hayloft. He had offered Jake a dollar and had it grumpily refused. "This place smell to you like the Broadwater in Helena, Ry?" Jake had asked. "It ain't a hotel, so there ain't no charge."

Likely he should have taken Jake's attitude as an inkling of how the town would receive one Riley Buckner, late of Deer Lodge. As he ate his breakfast, he began to understand. Any small town trial was held many times —once in the courtroom and before and after at the saloons and on the street corners. Whatever judgment had thus been reached in his case had not been wholly against him. Naturally there was restraint! Who would want to slap him on the back saying, "Ry, old hoss, where you bin keepin' yourself?"

He warmed, realizing this and remembering that the jury had recommended leniency. Last night he had thought the townspeople would no longer care about him. Now he began recalling a hundred kindnesses during his boyhood. A four-bit meal spread on someone's table after a ten-cent chopping stint in the woodshed. A garment handed over as a cast-off when some youngster of the family might have worn it. He had been wrong last night, for these people were not lost to him.

A package of food under his arm, he came out to the street again and looked at the bustle of the morning—bonneted shoppers here and there—horses flicking their tails at hitch-racks—a boy rolling a hoop, a spotted pup gamboling at his heels. Not far away, Prudence Lane swept the porch of her mother's mercantile. A horseman rode by, and he noted the Boxed J brand before he lifted his eyes and identified the rider. Billy Larb. Old hellfire and brimstone Billy.

He saw Billy dismount before the mercantile, speak to Pru, and the two go inside. Some routine errand for Boxed J, likely. Some little thing to be bought, though the owner's son lay hidden today, a fugitive, and the clods were probably now falling on the coffin of the man he'd killed. Life went on. Men fought and died, and in the wake of turmoil came more turmoil and anguish and the flowering of dark ambitions. But still, if, say, an awl got broken and was needed for the mending of harness, someone went to a store to get a new one.

He might go over to the mercantile himself and say

hello to Maw Lane and have a few more words with Pru, but the awl he needed was somewhere else.

He crossed back to the livery and found gnarled little Jake Hollis returned to his cubby-hole, the whiskey reek of his breath betraying what need had taken him away earlier. He told Jake, "I want to rent a horse and gear. For how long I don't know."

Jake had been a working cowhand till rheumatism had got hold of him. He had never been known to speak a kind word or do a harsh deed. "Take your pick," he said. "You'll find gear around. You got no hooks in your pants."

Buckner nodded. "Sure, Jake. Got a six-shooter I could have the loan of?"

Jake indicated the packing case that was his bureau. "Half a dozen in there. Belts, holsters, shells, too. Some cowhand comes in, wants a buggy to go sparkin' some piece of calico. Leaves his gun in place of rent, says he'll square up come payday. Next I hear, he's married the calico, moved to Nevady, and they've got four kids, two of 'em in school. The damn' fools figger I'm in the gun-collectin' business."

Buckner swept away the ragged burlap curtaining the box. He picked out a belt, a holster, enough shells to fill the belt, and a bone-handled Colt forty-five. He strapped on the belt.

Jake regarded him dourly. "If I didn't loan you that iron, you'd get one somewheres else anyway. For the record, though, I'm sayin' here and now that I like Duke Jordan. He has his faults, but I like him."

"Got it all figured out I'm going after his scalp, eh?"

"One of two things fetched you back, Ry. If you'd

asked the loan of a shovel, I'd figgered you was goin'
diggin' a certain carpetbag. But you crave a gun, which
means it's a man you're huntin'."

"Jake, it was hinted at my trial that I'd get off a lot
easier if I'd tell where I'd hidden the rest of Gulley's
money. I couldn't make the deal, because I didn't steal
that money. But you still could be guessing wrong. I
might be needing this gun against Hatchet—or Virg
McQueen."

He left abruptly and went out among the stalls and
selected a horse, picking a lumpy gelding that would
last in hill country. He began saddling, annoyed by the
talk he'd just had with Hollis. Too many people were
jumping to conclusions. Too many either wanted to
choose a side or had already figured out which side he'd
be on. Spence Rigby in the back room of the Frontier
last night. Sam Tull. McQueen in the empty courtroom.
And now Jake.

He rode into the street and headed west. At the edge
of Signal, he looked back and could see the cemetery,
with the flatbed wagon up there, and the men of
Hatchet grouped with heads bowed. Soon now they
would be riding.

He had to make time while the edge was still his, yet
again he must make haste slowly. A couple of miles
beyond Signal the gulch ended, and the valley spread
before him, vast and hill-rimmed, the dun distances un-
dulating to foothill and mountain barrier where blue of
fir and gold of aspen swept upward to rocky baldness.
Seeing this, he was truly come home; but today all of
space became a challenge. Where, in far flung vista, did
Duke hide? He remembered McQueen's idea of last

night: that a Riley Buckner, knowing Duke so well, would know where Duke would head. He tried putting himself in Duke's boots.

Had Duke really run? Or was Duke forted up at Boxed J right now, knowing that old Gulley would stand off Sheriff McQueen and Hatchet and the state militia if necessary? No, Duke was too decent for that. Duke would know that such a stand would mean capture in the long run, with his father's life endangered. Duke would have run, all right, drawing trouble away from the ranch.

But where? North to the Canadian border, nearly the width of Montana away? South to the mountain spine between Montana and Idaho, or even farther south toward Mexico? The nets would be thrown in all directions, as Duke would very well know. McQueen's first move had likely been to get on the railroad telegraph and send the word to lawmen everywhere to be on the lookout for Duke. Duke's choice, then, would have been to flee from home yet stay reasonably close. The better to have access to grub and any other supplies he'd need. The better to be in touch with what was going on.

The hills would be hiding Duke. The more he tried putting himself in Duke's boots, the more he grew certain of that. The wild, tangled hills that would be nearly deserted now, with the herds of the several ranches brought down from their summer pasturage a month ago, the hills with their abandoned mines and crumbling shacks and forgotten prospect holes, their myriad places to hide a man.

Thinking these things, he had ridden on, following a

wagon road between boulders and high banks and stunted trees. This was the road to Boxed J, the closest of the ranches to town, and he quit the road and cut overland toward the Garnets, making the high lift of Table Mountain his beacon. And so he faced the hills as Duke must have faced them last night, and the search was both narrowed and made great, for the hills might take weeks of combing. Never mind. There would be sign somewhere, sign lost in the traveled valley but plainly read in the emptier reaches, a curl of campfire smoke, a fresh hoofprint of a shod horse where only game might be expected to roam, a rider skylined on a ridge in some unwary moment. No matter how careful Duke might be, sooner or later there would be sign.

He wondered if he had taken Duke's trail too poorly prepared. He had wanted the edge of time against Hatchet, but maybe he should have rented a packhorse and fetched a supply of grub and camping gear. But he'd make out. The package of food in the saddlebag would last him a while, and he could get meals at the scattered ranches. And he could sleep where Duke would likely sleep, in some old shack or mine shaft, or in the cave.

The cave!

He almost jerked the horse to a halt. Why hadn't it struck him before? The cave, of course! That hole in the hills he and Duke had found when they were ten and used as their secret place till they had put boyhood behind them. The cave of many sunny afternoons where sometimes they had played pirate, planning the sack of Panama, and sometimes smugglers, and often Indians, watching for unwary wagon trains. There they had once attempted the blood-brother ritual of Indians, having heard of such, and had clumsily cut their arms and tried making the blood mingle. They had had to hurry to old Doc Fargo in town, who had kept a straight face while predicting blood poisoning and amputation, scaring the liver out of them.

Duke might have remembered the cave. And Duke might be thinking that nearly everyone would have forgotten that the cave had been their hang-out in those years long ago.

He looked to the hills again. He had held only to the general direction of Table Mountain, but now he pulled the horse in a line for the old Brewster place. That and the grass-grown road beyond it that climbed toward the cave.

He wanted to gallop, for he was suddenly impatient with the miles, but it was no country for hard riding. Look at the spread of the valley and it seemed flat as a carpet, but there were ridges and coulees and winding creeks, enough up-and-down to remind a man of the old boast that if Montana were flattened out, it would be bigger than Texas. He had to pick a careful way, sometimes following coulees where chokecherries hung black from frost, sometimes riding ridges from which he had far glimpses of grazing cattle. All the miles were hard won.

Then, topping still another ridge, he sighted a rider ahead.

Some Pothook cowhand, he supposed, for Pothook pressed against the foothills hereabouts. The rider dropped over a rise and would have been lost to thought as well as sight except that his next glimpse, twenty minutes later, showed that he'd shortened the distance between them; and he got a better look. A girl, wearing one of those divided skirts. He thought instantly of Dorcas last night and grew almost certain it was Dorcas ahead. Dorcas hunting Duke? Dorcas, who had been both his girl and Duke's, now trying to help Duke in his trouble?

Excitement stirred in him. He became cautious, making sure to keep hidden lest she chance to look back, yet keeping on her line of travel. She, too, seemed to be headed toward the old Brewster place. He grew even more careful. Before crossing any ridge, he dismounted and crawled to where he could look ahead. He lost track of time, knowing only that the day was deep into afternoon. He crawled one more ridge and saw the Brewster house, a two-story ruin, in the hollow below him. Before the house the girl was dismounting.

He lay watching her. She let her reins fall, and with her horse ground-anchored, she began pacing up and down, switching at her skirt with her quirt. She looked this way and that; patiently she awaited someone, and his excitement grew. Finally she looked toward the ridge where he lay; and with her face turned fully toward him, he had the shock of disappointment. It was Pru, not Dorcas, he had been following.

He moved back to his horse, mounted, and came boldly over the ridge and rode down the slant into the yard. She watched his coming, and when he was close enough, he touched the brim of his hat and said, "Hello, Pru."

"Hello, Ry," she said, and the greeting was warm, but a shadow lay in her eyes, not of fear or alarm but of worry, and he guessed that his coming had put it there. He recalled Billy Larb's riding into town and accosting her on the mercantile porch. She must have hit the trail at once to have been ahead of him. Probably she'd ridden out while he'd been arranging with Jake Hollis for a horse and gear and a gun. Maybe Billy Larb hadn't come to town for an awl or some rock salt or whatever of a score of things Boxed J might have needed. Maybe Billy had brought her a message.

He saw no sense in sparring. "Pru," he asked, "would you be here because of Duke?"

He had realized last night that she had become a pretty girl. He saw now that she was as pretty as Dorcas, but in a different way. Dorcas had a cool blonde beauty. Pru's was a warmer loveliness. This he noted with one corner of his mind; his real concern was with his question.

She turned as intense as at their parting last night. "Ry, you were wondering what was going on around Signal. I told you all I knew at the time, about the Strip and Lark Rigby's threat. This morning I heard the rest of it—how Lark got killed by Duke Jordan. You were in town, so you must have heard it, too. You're hunting Duke, aren't you?"

"I'm hunting Duke."

"To see him in prison or hanged because Boxed J put you in prison, Ry?"

He had been annoyed with Jake Hollis; he was more annoyed now. Did everyone believe that no greater need could drive a man than the need for vengeance? And with this latest annoyance, he was also hurt. Whatever he had expected from Pru Lane, he had not expected this. He swung down from the saddle. "Pru," he said, "I told you last night I was looking for something I lost five years ago. Isn't that good enough?"

"And I told you to go away because there's nothing here for you. It's still not too late."

He had a flash of understanding. "Was your concern with me, Pru? Or with Duke, or Dorcas, or both of them? Why did you hesitate when I asked you where Dorcas was? She was in town, Pru. I got a glimpse of her afterwards. At the courthouse with Oliver Landers."

Her eyes dropped, and she flicked at her boot with the quirt. Then she looked up at him. "All right, Ry," she said. "You're bound to find out a few things anyway, if you stay around here. Dorcas lives at Boxed J now. She works there."

"Works there?"

"Keeping books, Ry. She's been out there about two months now. I told you that Lark Rigby came to Maw yesterday and said he couldn't be trading with us any more, considering. That was because real trouble was shaping between Hatchet and Boxed J, and one of the Lane family is with Boxed J now."

"But what has that got to do with me?"

She bit at her lower lip. "I guess you'll have to have it square between the eyes, Ry." She took a note from her pocket and unfolded it. "Billy Larb fetched this to me about noon. It's from Dorcas. It says, 'Ride out to the old Brewster place as soon as you can, but don't let anyone know where you are going, or why. I'll meet you there and hope to have a preacher and a second witness come, too. I am marrying Duke today. Please trust me and do as I say.' "

He heard the message, but at the end a red haze was swimming before his eyes and Pru's voice had become a blur. He knew now what business Dorcas must have had at the courthouse with Oliver Landers. A marriage license! He said, "So that's why she quit writing me at Deer Lodge!"

Pru put the note away. "I didn't want to do this to you, Ry."

He found himself trembling, and he stared at her without really seeing her. "I only wanted to look Duke Jordan straight in the eye and ask him a question," he said. "I wanted him to tell me whether he framed me into prison, and if so, why. After that, I would know what I'd have to do. But now he's got two things to account for. Stuck behind bars, did I have a chance against him with Dorcas?"

She came close and clutched at the lapels of his coat. "Ry," she said, "I didn't understand! You were giving him the benefit of the doubt, but now I've shaken that. Ry, think! Can you be sure when you blame him? Is it Duke marrying Dorcas—or is it Dorcas marrying Duke?"

"The same thing, Pru."

He saw a startled look cross her face, and he thought it came from what he had said or what his own face must be showing. Then he realized she was looking beyond him toward the ridge. He turned to see riders skylined above, a dozen of them. Hatchet! He damned himself for an incompetent. He had been too intent on trailing Pru to watch his backtrail, and Hatchet had sighted him, and he had become the hunter hunted. He sprang away from Pru as dirt gouted near his feet. The hills caught the sharp report of a six-shooter and sent it echoing.

7 : **Deadlocked**

Say this for danger, it swept a man's mind clean of everything but the need to get to cover. Buckner moved fast. No time now for thinking of Dorcas and Duke, or even to wonder how Hatchet dared try open, unprovoked gun-play. Pru's horse, nearby, pitched and then bolted; and the livery stable mount began rearing. Buckner snatched at the reins. He got hold of them and pulled at the horse, bringing the mount between him and Hatchet. He shouted at Pru, "Get into the house!"

The gun spoke again. He heard the high, thin whine of the bullet. Pru turned and darted for the ruin behind them. Buckner's horse pitched and broke free and went galloping toward the valley, hard after Pru's mount. Buckner freed his borrowed gun from leather and flung a shot at Hatchet, not even aiming. Pru had gained the house. He went sprinting after her. A plank in the rotted porch broke under him, and he nearly fell. He lunged through the front doorway.

This Brewster place had been a cow ranch once, a small spread started by an Iowa family who had gone broke during the hard winter six years ago. The house showed the impracticality of the owners, reflecting the town trend toward frame rather than log and having two stories. The porch was a Midwestern affectation. This was Brewster's monument, this weather-warped ruin. The glass had long since gone from the windows, the doors from their hinges, taken for kindling by overnight occupants who had built their campfires in the yard, and cows had strayed in and out of the building. But the walls were sturdy, and the place some better than no fortress at all.

Pru stood with her back to a wall, breathing hard, made prettier by excitement and showing no panic. Buckner flung himself to the parlor floor and elbowed his way toward the big front window which looked to the ridge. He batted off his hat and raised himself to peer out, expecting to draw a shot, expecting to see the full force of Hatchet charging down the slope.

They were still up there. They were bunched around Tull, and it was he who held a smoking six-shooter. Spence Rigby was doing the talking, leaning forward in his saddle and thrusting his jaw at Tull. Tull made reply, pointing down at the house and waving his gun. The rumble of the voices reached below, but the words were a blur of sound carrying no meaning but the intimation of argument. Buckner began to understand. They had sighted him, even as he had sighted Pru, and they had trailed him, but it had been Tull alone who had let his wrath run wild. Rigby was too careful for that. Rigby was trying now to persuade Tull from his anger.

Pru asked, low voiced, "Are they coming?"

"Council of war," Buckner said. "Keep back there!"

"How did they dare shoot at us?" she demanded. "We're not Duke, wanted for murder. Have they gone crazy?"

"Only Tull," he said. "Rigby wants Duke, not me. Last night Rigby was willing to have me taught a lesson, short of killing me. That's why I was on the run when I climbed through your bedroom window. After that I bucked them a second time. It's got personal with Tull. I'm sorry you got mixed into it again."

"They'll ride on," she said. "They'll not want to answer to the sheriff for this."

"I wonder, Pru. I happen to know that McQueen doesn't stack very high in their eyes. Still, the law is the law. Rigby will be remembering that. I'm not so sure about Tull."

Pru started to speak again.

"Hush, now!" he said. "They're moving."

Hatchet, strung out in single file with Rigby up front, walked their horses along the ridge, headed toward the hills. All but Tull. He still held his horse in check; and as the others moved away from him, he looked after them fixedly, then looked down into the hollow where the house stood; and in that moment he seemed to make up his mind. He put his horse off the crest and came galloping down the slant, and as he came, he fired.

Buckner heard the solid *thunk* of the bullet in the siding of the house. It made challenge enough. He lifted himself, fired at Tull, and knew that he had missed. Tull, neck-reining the horse, drove it in a zigzag fashion, veering hard to the left as he came thundering into the yard. He passed from sight.

Buckner, scrambling across the floor on hands and knees, got to a window in the south wall. Here he had a view of what remained of Brewster's barn and the tumbled-down corrals beside it. Tull was nowhere to be seen, which meant Tull had gone into that wreck of a barn. Then the man appeared, long and gaunt, bursting from the barn doorway. Buckner sent a bullet at him. Out there in the yard stood a pump and platform beside a watering trough. Tull flung himself behind the trough and almost instantly raised to fire at the window where Buckner crouched. Then the man bobbed out of sight again.

"Sam!" Buckner shouted. "Call off this damn' fool business!"

Tull's voice came, cold, dispassionate, deadly. "Last night you made me look down the throat of a gun, Buckner. You had the edge then. But nobody does that to me and lives. Now come out and fight."

"Pru Lane's here," Buckner called back. "You know that. What about her?"

"She doesn't figure one way or the other. This is between us, Buckner."

From that far wall, Pru said, "He's lying, Ry. I *do* figure. I've got to."

Of course she did. A man could die here today, Buckner realized, and the law would look into this little affair if one did. That was what Spence Rigby had understood, and that was why Rigby had ridden on, taking Hatchet with him. If the man who died were Riley Buckner, there would be Pru to testify that the fight had been forced on him, making Sam Tull a murderer. And thus if Riley Buckner died, Prudence Lane had to die, too.

That was how it added up, and damned if it didn't make a real predicament. Buckner shook his head. That news of Duke and Dorcas about to be married had made him see red at the very moment Hatchet had appeared. Now there was someone to fight, but he had to think of Pru. Already he hated the rough planking under his knees, the heat and moldering smell of this old house. He wanted to go through the window and charge at Tull as Tull wished, but he couldn't. And so he stayed crouched, waiting for Tull to raise for a shot and thus present some small target; and Tull hid out there, waiting the same chance at him.

He kept his eyes on that watering trough, worrying about Pru the while. They could both slip through one of the windows on the north side of the house, he supposed, but beyond was a stand of cottonwoods and a deep carpet of fallen leaves that would crunch underfoot, betraying them. Let Tull suspect that they had fled, and the man would be after them, with the advantage of having a horse while they would be afoot.

No good, he decided. Still, he could let Pru escape in that direction while he kept Tull pinned down behind the trough. But suppose Tull moved too fast for him and got at Pru. Tull, throwing that first shot from the ridge when he and Pru had been standing close together, had proved he had no concern for Pru's life. Remembering this, he shook his head. Pru would be safer behind walls. He couldn't stand having any harm come to Pru.

Tull tore him from his thinking by raising up and

firing a hasty shot. He fired back at Tull, his bullet splintering wood from the edge of the trough. Instantly he was sorry. Tull had likely goaded him to that response just to make sure the house was still occupied.

He waited for Tull to try again. He kept waiting. Afternoon must soon be giving away to twilight. Surely it was an hour now since Hatchet had appeared on the ridge. Fretting, he suddenly remembered that according to Dorcas's note, she would be coming here. The thought panicked him. Dorcas would ride right into this! Then he remembered that she'd be bringing a preacher and a second witness. Quite a different matter. Even a man as headstrong as Tull would hesitate at mass murder. But still he worried. And still the afternoon droned on, with nothing changing. Again he wanted to go through the window and charge at Tull, and again he decided he didn't dare. The advantage would be Tull's, and what of Pru?

Tull broke the silence. "Come out, you yellow-bellied jailbird," Tull shouted. No anger in his voice, only that cold deadliness. "Come out and make a fight the way a man would."

"Nothing doing, Tull."

"It's getting on to dark, Buckner. I'll smoke you out then. Once I can move from here, I'll touch a match to the house."

He's bluffing, Buckner thought, but he wasn't sure. To gauge what a man might do, you first had to have the measure of the man. "A bigger brute than you, Spence," McQueen had said of Sam Tull last night. Tull, the Texan, dour specimen of that rollicking breed, hated by his own kind. Tull, who had worked for Lark

Rigby by sufferance because he was a top hand with cattle. Tull the relentless, a man obstinate enough to have stayed here to make his fight despite any persuasion of Spence Rigby. Yes, Tull would use a torch when the chance came.

And still there was Pru to think about, Pru so quiet there by the wall through the long waiting, the deadlock. Should he urge her to slip away by a north window and try covering her? Whatever was done must be done before darkness closed down. Tull's threat had made that plain.

Suddenly he cocked an ear, listening hard. He heard a crow caw not far away. He heard the fallen leaves of the cottonwood rustle beneath a light breeze. But he heard something else, faint with distance, the racketing of hoofs, the grind of wagon wheels. Hope ran through him, sharp as a lance. "Pru!" he whispered hoarsely. "Do you hear it? North! Go see who's coming!"

That sound grew out of the valley, up the road that led here to the Brewster place and then climbed on into the hills. Pru darted away, being careful not to pass any window commanded by Tull's gun. Buckner could hear the growing thunder of sound. A wagon, pulled by a team, he decided. At least three other horses as well.

Pru came back into the room. "A covered wagon," she reported. "Two people on the seat. There's a rider alongside the wagon, leading two saddle horses. Ours, I think, caught up somewhere."

"Good!" he said. He put on his hat. He looked through the window just in time to see Tull rise from behind the trough and start running toward the barn. Tull had heard the thunder, too, and though the house cut off his view, he'd been able to guess at the size of the force arriving. Now, with Tull up and running, the edge was Buckner's, and he went through the window and after Tull. The man heard the beat of boots behind him, for he turned and threw a shot. Buckner felt the air lash of it. He fell behind the watering trough, on the opposite side from where Tull had hidden. He laid his gun across the edge and fired, but Tull got into the barn.

The man appeared almost instantly, mounted and at a gallop, clinging to one side of his horse Comanche style and firing under the neck. The bullets went wide, but they kept Buckner pinned down. Then Tull rounded the barn and headed on into the foothills in the direction Hatchet had taken.

Buckner reared up. He ran forward and reached the road and got a glimpse of Tull spurring hard, but the distance was now too great for six-shooter use. He turned. Roaring up came the covered wagon, a man at the lines, a younger man beside him. Flanking the wagon was Boxed J's Billy Larb, and he was indeed leading the two horses that had bolted with the first gunfire.

Larb said, astonished, "Ry Buckner! Didn't figure to find you here."

"Hello, Billy," Buckner said. "Believe me, man, I'm glad to see you!"

Pru came from the house. She stood on the porch, fair and slim in the last sunlight, and she put her hand to one of the supports to steady herself. Only then did she show what this afternoon had taken out of her.

Buckner looked at the wagon and its riders. On the

canvas of the side nearest him, words had been smeared with axle grease. JUDGE NOT, THAT YE BE NOT JUDGED. The man at the lines was a preacher if he'd ever seen one, a lanky scarecrow dressed in rusty black. The younger man looked like the older with thirty years sheared away. Buckner nodded at them. "I don't believe I know you," he said.

"Jones," the older man said. "The Reverend Gideon Jones. This is my son Tobias."

Larb said to Pru, "Dorcas asked me to find him and head him here, him and his boy. The reverend is a rover, new to these parts. He didn't know the way to the Brewster place, so I came along. A couple miles back, we found these horses strayed. I recognized one as yours, miss, the other from Jake Hollis's stable. We were fetching them along, holding to an easy gait, till we heard gunshots. Then we came at a gallop. Wasn't that Sam Tull just rode off?"

"A private fight," Buckner said, thinking with wry humor that it had been three men of peace who had saved him, a preacher, his son, and a prayer-meeting cowpoke. "Trouble was, Pru might have got killed."

Larb looked around. "Dorcas said she'd meet the reverend here."

"She hasn't come yet," Pru said.

Larb shoved back his hat and scratched his head. "I should be home at Boxed J. And the reverend can't wait long, either. He has promised to conduct prayers with one of the west-end ranch families this evening. We can stay awhile, I suppose."

Buckner walked to his horse and took the reins from Larb. "I'm obliged, Billy," he said. "I'll be getting along." He swung up into the saddle and lifted his hand to Pru. "You'll be safe now. Safer than with me around. I'm mighty sorry you got caught up in a grudge against me."

He neck-reined the horse about and headed it along the ancient road toward the hills. He had walked the mount no more than a hundred feet when he heard Pru call after him. He turned and saw her come running from the porch. He waited till she reached his stirrup.

"Ry," she asked, "where are you going?"

He looked back at the wagon and the rider beside it. Larb and the two Joneses were talking, out of earshot. He looked at Pru. "Riding," he said. "You've got everybody here who's needed for a wedding party except the bride and groom. A preacher. The legal number of witnesses, plus one. But Duke isn't going to show up at any place as open as this without having a look first. Not today. And not if his old friend Ry Buckner is in sight. Likely he and Dorcas heard the shooting and are somewhere back in the hills. But maybe they'll come down now. And maybe I can meet him on the way."

Pru shook her head. "So you've come full circle, Ry, back to where you were when Hatchet showed on the ridge and the shooting started. As I was saying then, you were giving Duke the benefit of the doubt, but I shook your faith in him."

"Just the same," he said, "I'm grateful to you. You wanted me to get out before I learned how things stand between Duke and Dorcas. I appreciate your trying to spare me."

"Oh, Ry, I'm not your guardian angel! You've got big enough shoulders. It's just that I like you, Ry; I always have. You put in five years in prison. Some of us believe you didn't deserve that. Anyway, I figured you'd been hurt enough by all that's happened."

He felt uncomfortable. "I've already told you I'm grateful, Pru."

"That's not the point!" She was growing more distressed. "I'm not concerned with what you might do to Duke. He's got big shoulders, too. I'm concerned with what you may do to yourself. Even now your face looks different from when you rode here this afternoon. Older. Harder. I don't believe it was that round with Sam Tull that made it so. I put another strike against Duke in your mind."

"All the more reason I've got to find him," he said stiffly.

"To have it out—with guns?"

He shook his head. "If that had been my notion, I'd have fetched a gun with me when I came home, girl. All right, I've got one now, to use where I need it. The only difference between now and earlier is what I already told you. Duke's got two things instead of one to account for."

He lifted the reins and touched the horse with his heel. He didn't look at Pru as he rode away. He faced toward the hills again, the first red flame of anger dead within him but in its place something cold and heavy and persistent, the cinder of wrath.

8 : **Three on the Trail**

Strong in Dorcas had grown the feeling that she was being followed. Mustn't let this panic her, she had told herself. Mustn't keep glancing back as she'd done a dozen times in the last hour. She dismounted and picked a few chokecherries and ate them, acting for all the world like someone idling through a lazy afternoon with no particular destination. While she was at this, she glanced casually in all directions and listened hard for the clop of hoofs on her backtrail. She saw nothing alarming, heard nothing. But just as she swung up to her saddle again, she caught a glint of light on a far ridge to the northeast.

That was the direction from which she had come. Hours behind lay Boxed J and her start of late morning. Someone back there with field glasses? Someone keeping track of her and at the same time staying a good distance behind? She thought of Abe Lofstrum's vigil of last night; she supposed that Hatchet might have a net of riders flung across the valley today. But more likely Hatchet would be in the hills, knowing that Duke wouldn't be boldly riding the valley. She thought of Dad Jordan, who had asked her a question regarding Duke's whereabouts and got half an answer.

Nothing to do but ride on and hope to give her follower the slip. She had crossed half the valley, and before her lay piled the foothills that kowtowed to mighty Table Mountain; she was somewhere on Pothook's vast acreage now, in a still land of coulee and draw and ridge. She mustn't make her pursuer warier by letting him know she'd grown worried about her backtrail. Whoever the man was, he might be assuming that she rode now to meet Duke; but regardless, to shake off the fellow, she had first to throw him off guard.

On a flat bit of meadowland she came upon a couple of dozen head of grazing cattle, fat Herefords, for Pothook had taken to upgrading its stock after that hard winter of horrible memory. She picked her way through the small herd, the cows eyeing her stolidly. She hoped no Pothook rider was nearby. She had carefully skirted Pothook's buildings a few miles back, for she had a bedroll tied behind her saddle, and those blankets didn't square with the fiction of the aimless ride. No sense in arousing curiosity needlessly, even if the questions in men's eyes would remain unasked out of politeness.

Best to avoid people, and best to keep to cover wherever possible. Precious little cover here, though, in this naked meadowland. Overhead clouds rode, laying their smoky shadows in a mottled pattern across the brown grass, and the hills showed soft and blue and golden in the afternoon sunlight. Another day she would have thrilled to the scene with its great sweep of distances, its sunlight and shadow, its autumn colors. Now she rode fretful, wanting only to reach the hills yet not daring to, not with someone close at her heels.

She pushed on through the cattle and began climbing a rise. She saw a rider then, quartering toward her. He came out of the east, and she told herself he couldn't be the man with the field glasses. Not enough time for that one to have maneuvered to where this fellow rode. Some Pothook hand, likely, and there'd be no avoiding him without deliberately doing so and thus making her presence all the more obvious. She rode on, and as the rider drew nearer she recognized him as Sheriff Virgil McQueen. No mistaking that lean figure nor the color-less garb that made him one with sagebrush and dun grassland. Now she even made out the implacable face beneath the tugged-down hat brim.

She drew in her breath sharply. If she had to name the one man above all she did not want to meet today, he would be Virgil McQueen. He pulled his horse to a stop, blocking her. She brought her own mount to a stand, having no choice. He said, "Afternoon, Dorcas," and touched his hat brim. He seemed to be looking at nothing in particular, yet she felt his eyes search her, felt them touch and hold on that bedroll.

"Afternoon, Virg," she said. She had known him since her childhood and grown up as much in awe of him as of any man. He was no Oliver Landers to be melted with a smile.

"Might you be on your way to Duke?" he asked.

To a lesser man she would have made denial, wrap-ping that denial in whatever lie-of-necessity seemed best suited to convince. To McQueen she said, "Not now, Virg. Not with you set to tag along."

"I'll find him anyway," he said. "Just a matter of time. Why don't you shorten it for me?"

This startled her. "You know whose side I'm on, Virg. Duke Jordan is the man I'm going to marry."

He nodded. "I know. Oliver Landers came to me just before I cleared town this morning. The word had got around about what Duke did last night. Oliver thought I ought to know about the marriage license."

"Just the same, I know the law," she said. "It was revised in 'eighty-seven and still stands, and there is not a word that prevents a marriage because one of the parties happens to be on the run. You can't stop me from marrying Duke."

"Wouldn't figure to try," he said. "Fact is, I might even help. Everybody's got a thing they're after, girl. Sometimes you find a person whose need aims the same direction as your own. I'm thinking we could help each other."

"I don't see how," she said.

He hooked a leg around his saddlehorn and got out brown papers and Bull Durham and began to shape up a cigarette. He might have had all the time in the world; and watching him Dorcas felt herself tighten, fearful of his aplomb. He sealed the cigarette with his tongue and touched fire to the tobacco and made very sure the match was extinguished before he dropped it into the grass.

"I recollect the first time I ever saw you to know who you really were," he said conversationally. "I was new to Signal then, and new to this sheriff's badge, and you couldn't have been over eight or nine years old. I'd met your maw at some kind of social doings and knew she was a widow with two little girls and had a store in a shack on Bottom Street, some smaller than the mercantile she's got now."

"Get on with it," she said.

"Came a winter evening, and I met up with a little girl tugging a sled along the wagon road just west of town. She had a gunny-sack on that sled, and in that gunny-sack was coal. Some miners were working a seam of coal they'd struck, and they were having the coal hauled to town by wagon. Sometimes they heaped the wagon too high and a little coal would shake off onto the road. You'd been picking up that coal."

"I remember," she said. "I used to make faces and shout names at the driver, hoping I could anger him into throwing a piece of coal at me—a big piece. But instead, he always smiled and waved."

"You were too pretty to have coal throwed at you, girl, so the driver never caught on. I can picture you plain, all eyes and golden hair and sort of starved looking. I asked you what you had in the sack; and you looked up at the badge on my coat, and told me plain what you'd picked up; and you made it plain, too, that you'd earned it, not stolen it. But the thing I remember most is what you said next. You recollect?"

She was struggling back through the mists of memory to the night of which he spoke, and she could feel the cold again and her tiredness, but still she couldn't be sure whether she recalled their meeting or whether his talk had recreated it for her. She only knew that a forgotten pain had been harked up, a forgotten humiliation.

So many times she had gone along that road with sled or wagon, depending on the season! She remembered how the other girls her age had made fun of her because of those excursions. She remembered how once, after such a trip, she had hastily changed into her best frock and hurried to a birthday party for one of the Galloway sisters, and she could hear again the shrill voice of her hostess saying, "Why, Dorcas! You've got a smear of coal dust on your cheek!"

"You recollect what you said to me?" McQueen persisted.

"I—I'm not sure."

"You looked me square in the eye. 'When I grow up, I'll never have to hunt coal,' you said. 'I'll be rich, and other people will haul it for me.'"

"All right," she said stiffly. "So I grew up, but I didn't become rich. What are you getting at, Virg?"

"At what it will mean to you to marry Duke Jordan."

Anger flared in her. "You think it's Boxed J I'm after. You think it's that alone. You think exactly what Dad Jordan will think when he learns I bought that license last night."

"I think," he said calmly, "that you make your head rule you, not your heart. It was as easy to fall in love with the son of Boxed J's owner as with any other man. Now wasn't it?"

"Yes, Virg," she said honestly. "That's right."

He carefully pinched out the cigarette he had been smoking. He nodded toward the bedroll she carried. "Duke must have left mighty fast last night. Too fast to pick up the blankets he'll be needing. I'm guessing that in your saddlebags you've got extra grub and maybe his razor and a few other possibles. Take them to him. And take a message from me at the same time. Will you do that?"

"I'm listening," she said cautiously.

"Tell him the only story I got on what happened between him and Lark Rigby last night came from Sam Tull and had to be one-sided. Just the same, after sleeping on the situation, I see a chance for him. I'm no lawyer. My job is to bring a man in, not to try him. But I think Duke's got a good chance in court whether Lark got a gun out of leather or not. You see, any man who was cutting a Boxed J fence was trespassing, and Duke had a right to defend Jordan property, even with a gun. Tell him that."

"I'm supposed to talk him into giving himself up? Is that what you expect?"

"Look at it sharp, girl. The longer Duke hides out, the more trouble he makes for the law. And the more trouble he makes, the less chance he has of getting the law to be lenient. Can't you see how much better his case will be if he rides in and surrenders?"

She sat quiet, thinking, thinking. Last night she had looked at the situation exactly as Duke had, that a man lay dead and the one who had felled him wore a murderer's brand, considering. She had flung her mind down that channel of thought, and murder had stayed murder, with no consideration of any other possibility. For the first time since Duke had paced the kitchen, pouring out his incoherent story, she caught a glimmer of hope. There *was* a chance! McQueen had just pointed it out.

"Let's suppose he comes in and stands trial," McQueen went on. "And let's suppose the jury decides the shooting was justified. The two of you can be married in your mother's parlour then. Not hidden out somewhere, ready to jump at the cracking of a twig."

"All right, Virg. I'll tell him." She looked at McQueen for a long, calculating moment. "But there's one thing he'll likely ask, for it's in my own mind. You talked about everybody having something they're after. Maybe we could help each other, you said. Duke might want to know what you figure to gain besides saving yourself a chase all over the hills that could add up to weeks."

"My gain?" Now it was his turn to be thoughtful, calculating. "I'd reckoned you'd guessed. I want an end to trouble."

"Sheriffs live on trouble," she said. "It gives them talking points when election time comes."

"Trouble, girl, is only a man's stock in trade when he's young enough to handle it."

For a second she wondered if she'd heard him right. McQueen afraid? McQueen putting his fear into words? But the very fact that he had was the measure of his need. Too old, they were saying, and she had heard the whispers and discredited them, knowing that any man in office as long as Virgil McQueen tallied up as many enemies as friends. Now she fully understood why he had stopped her here in the hope of enlisting her aid. McQueen's real foe had been the silently marching years.

"Dorcas," he said, "I'm not going to pretend with you. I want to be re-elected. Here's Duke running the hills with me after him, and Hatchet after him, and Riley Buckner after him, too. Ah, I see you didn't know about Ry! Anyhow, there's apt to be guns and lynch ropes and trouble spreading like ripples from a rock dropped into water. Ten years ago I could have handled the whole mess; and the greater the trouble got, the bigger my name would have been afterwards. But now I want Duke Jordan to ride in and surrender. That won't put any shine to my name, but it won't put a strike against it, either. That's how things stack up as far as I'm concerned."

"I'll talk to him, Virg."

"And I'll give you your chance to get to him, girl. I'll not follow you. I'll even ride in the opposite direction. But I can only grant you twenty-four hours. After that, I'll have to hunt him down and bring him in."

"I'll get to him as soon as I can," she said. "I promise you that."

He dropped his foot to the stirrup. Facing away from the hills, he was about to ride past her when he stopped. She could see the puzzled expression in his eyes. "Dorcas," he asked, "what would Duke be wanting with writing paper and envelope and a pencil?"

Startled, she said, "I don't know. What do you mean?"

"I asked questions at a couple of the ranches today. Thought I might pick up something. At Pothook they'd seen Duke. Last night, late. He came to the bunkhouse and woke up Fred Marley. You'll recollect that Fred rode for Boxed J a couple of seasons back. Fred says

Duke seemed excited, nervous, but he didn't say anything about being in trouble. Claimed he was on his way to Jupiter City on Boxed J business and needed to drop off a letter along the way and had forgot to fetch paper and pencil. Fred gave him same."

"I don't know anything about that," she said. "I truly don't."

She could tell that he believed her. He shrugged, then took out his watch, snapped open the case, and had a look. "Five of four," he said. "Twenty-four hours, remember." He touched a spur to his horse and rode away.

She jogged her own horse and headed onward. When she looked back, McQueen was through those Pothook cattle and riding to the northeast. She was excited by all she had learned, especially about the prospect of Duke's standing a chance in court, but she mustn't let her excitement lessen her caution. McQueen would keep his word about not following her, she was sure. But there were three on the trail, she remembered, and she had to consider that rider with the field glasses. Dad Jordan, most likely. Perhaps she should have asked McQueen to scout him out and take him off her trail. But any man had a right to ride the valley.

She recalled her temptation of the morning to tell Dad Jordan everything so that they might work together in Duke's interest. She had kept silent because of the marriage license. Now there was the question of how the old man might feel about Duke's surrendering. She could guess how that would be. Dad Jordan still dwelt in a violent past. He would argue that Duke should stay a fugitive, standing off everyone at gunpoint in the old tradition if necessary. More than ever she must keep Dad Jordan from getting to Duke before she did.

First of all she must be married to Duke. She had known that when he'd told her of the shooting last night, and so she had gone at once to buy the license. Let the Dad Jordans and the Virgil McQueens see opportunism in that if they wished. Duke would be her husband, hunted or court-freed as the case might be, but far better that he be free. She had Pru waiting at the Brewster place, and possibly that preacher and his boy, who would make the second witness the law required. She could head for Brewsters' now, but not if Dad Jordan were following her. Or she could take a chance that Pru and the others would wait while she found Duke and brought him below.

Trouble was, she couldn't hurry to the cave. Instead, she must loiter, riding aimlessly until darkness came. Night would put her beyond reach of those field glasses that had glinted from a distant ridge.

Time to be moving again, Gulley Jordan knew, and mighty thankful he was for that. Rough on the belly lying stretched out here atop a cutbank, his elbows propped against the ground while he'd kept his field glasses glued to his eyes. He began backing down on hands and knees, not standing till he was sure he was far enough below the rim so that he wouldn't show. He stretched himself then, easing the ache in his back. Getting too old for climbing and crawling the way he'd done today, keeping a good distance behind that girl and having to pick her up from time to time with the glasses to be sure he hadn't lost her.

Scrambling to the bush where he had tied his horse, he hauled himself into the saddle with a groan. A lot more to think about than his aches, he realized. A mighty long talk that girl had had with Virg McQueen, and a mighty friendly one, seemed like, with Virg having himself a smoke and acting as if he had all day. The glasses had brought Virg close, plain to see, but all he'd got of the girl was her back. Made a man grind his teeth to see McQueen so clear and not be able to hear what he was saying.

Last glimpse, though, Virg had been heading this way, having angled from the direction in which he'd been riding when the glasses had first found him. Trick now was to get to cover before the sheriff reached here. Yonder a creek rolled down out of the hills to join the Garnet River farther to the west. A good stand of willows grew along the creek, and he headed his horse in that direction and pulled up in the willows. Here he dismounted and clamped a hand over his horse's nostrils to keep it from greeting McQueen's horse.

Presently McQueen came over a hump of land and rode on by. He watched McQueen as long as he was in sight; McQueen didn't so much as look over his shoulder. He frowned, speculating on McQueen. Any manhunter with McQueen's experience would surely have figured that Duke had hit for the Garnets. McQueen had been heading toward the hills before he met the girl; but after the talk, he'd faced in the opposite direction.

Now how did that add up? Maybe a lot of different

ways. But could it be that McQueen was leaving the hunt because that girl had promised to deliver the goods for him? Maybe a reward had been posted for Duke this morning. But, damn it, a woman wouldn't turn in her man. Still, now that he studied on it, he realized that one of the things he hadn't liked about Dorcas Lane was that she put so much store by money, and he'd begun to suspect that was why she'd set her cap for Duke. But Duke was outlawed now and not of much value in the marriage market, though maybe worth something on the hoof at the county seat. If Duke hadn't been sold out, then why had McQueen given up the hunt?

He climbed back into the saddle, troubled and angry. A lot of guessing he'd been doing, and likely he wasn't being fair; likely he was making a case against the girl because he didn't cotton to her. Just the same, he had more reason than before to stick to her trail, and he guessed he'd better be shortening the distance between them. Dark would be coming on, and he'd have to be close at her heels, or she'd give him the slip. He couldn't chance that now.

9 ⋮ Man Wounded

He had better be patient again, Riley Buckner decided. He had ridden hard through the foothills in the last daylight, and now the old Bellafonte mine road was leading him up Table Mountain, climbing, always climbing. Made no sense to push a horse against such terrain, and if he rode too fast he might overtake Hatchet's crew, which had to be somewhere ahead. Anger was a spur that could goad a man straight into trouble. Might as well face the fact that he had been driven by anger ever since Pru Lane had told him about the marriage plan. And those hours of being pinned down at the Brewster place by Sam Tull had only made his anger sharper.

A cool head was what he needed, not an angry heart. He must look calmly at this business of Duke and Dorcas planning marriage and see how the knowledge could help him find Duke. Earlier he had tried thinking as Duke would think and had thus got headed toward the cave. It still made sense that the cave was a likely hiding place for Duke. Pru had hinted that the marriage might be Dorcas's idea rather than Duke's. Suppose that were true. Then Dorcas, who had arranged to have a preacher and witnesses at the Brewster place, must have known where she could locate Duke. Since neither Dorcas nor Duke had showed up, Dorcas had either been delayed in reaching Duke or had been unable to persuade him to risk coming down to the Brewster place. Or perhaps Hatchet blocked them.

Speculation, all of this, but the cave was still worth looking into. Maybe he'd find not only Duke there but Dorcas as well. His jaw set. So be it. What he had to say could be said, regardless. Let Dorcas hear the question and the answer. Let Dorcas know what manner of man she intended marrying.

He had brought the horse to a walk. Twilight deepened into night, and he ate from the package of restaurant food he'd fetched in his saddlebag and drank from a creek near the roadside and headed on. Timber pressed him on either hand, and an eternity's needlefall made the underfooting spongy, and he rode in darkness, thankful that he knew this mountain so well. He had played here as a boy. He had trailed cattle up this slope as a young cowhand, for along here had moved Boxed J herds, including that one they had sold in Jupiter City five years ago for money that had never got to the ranch. A few miles above was the spot where his night camp had been attacked by a masked rider, and just beyond that was the abandoned Bellafonte.

Not so cold tonight, and not so windy, and the sky was clear, and there would be a moon later. Still, at this altitude the air was crisp, and he wished, as he had last night, for a warm coat. He might have borrowed one from Jake Hollis, he supposed. Well, it would be warm in the cave. Many a fire he and Duke had built within those walls.

He began watching the timber to his left carefully. After the first sharp climb from the foothills—the rise he had ascended so recklessly—Table Mountain lifted in a series of benches, these steps of a giant stairs broken by little meadows and long gulches running east and west. Soon now he would have to swing off the road and ride rock- and brush-choked Timmerman Gulch to the cave, which lay above a slope of shale at the gulch's far end. Trick now was to be careful not to pass the turnoff place in the darkness.

He saw the opening in the timber wall and pulled his horse into it, leaving the road. A trail led into the gulch, part of a maze of trails that criss-crossed the face of the mountain. He followed the trail through a rocky slot to where the gulch broadened and again he rode through timber. It was then he saw a fire ahead, flickering through the stand of pine and spruce. His first thought came fierce and triumphant: *Duke!* Instantly he knew better. Duke wouldn't be showing a fire now that he had become the pursued, little though this area might be traveled.

Then he knew, and knowing, damned his luck. Hatchet, of course! Hatchet up there ahead of him. He pulled his horse to a halt and considered. Perhaps he was wrong; perhaps some party of prospectors camped here. He dismounted and led the horse into timber, close to one of the rocky walls of the gulch. He tied up the animal and began making his way carefully through the trees in the direction of the fire.

He could go just so far and no farther. The timber thinned, and before him lay an open, grassy pocket. A good fifty yards from where he stood, the fire burned. A dozen men clustered around that fire, some standing, some hunkered on their heels; and he could see picketed horses in the farther rim of the firelight. Spence Rigby was recognizable among the men, big and paunchy and wearing the slicker he'd worn last night; and Sam Tull must have just overtaken the outfit, for he was here, too.

Luck came in two different packages, good and bad. Standing in the shadows and looking to where Hatchet had chosen to camp, Buckner knew which package he had drawn. Hatchet blocked the way to the cave. Yet this was no happenstance, for Hatchet's choice had been a natural one. A creek fed by springs flowed through the meadow; there was a spread of grass for grazing, and the walls of the gulch made shelter from the winds; it was altogether a fine camping place.

Hatchet had come prepared to spend at least one night in the open. He could see that, and he remembered he'd noticed a packhorse with the outfit on the ridge above Brewsters'. A coffee pot steamed over the fire, and a man was removing a frying pan from the flames while another man began passing tin plates around. Blankets were spread here and there.

How to get across that meadow and on up the gulch to the cave? Not much chance while Hatchet remained awake. Question then was whether they intended only an overnight stop here or whether this was to be the base camp while they searched the mountain. He had to know.

Dropping to his hands and knees, he crept closer. A few rocks were scattered about; a few bushes grew beyond the edge of the timber. He moved slowly from cover to cover, thankful that the babbling of the creek covered any sound he made. Yet that same mindless murmuring kept him from catching Hatchet's talk. He got within thirty yards of the fire, but still he couldn't hear what was being said. He lay behind a wildrose bush close to a low-growing juniper, not daring to approach nearer.

Rigby ate from a tin plate now. Tull had got a plate and was helping himself from the frying pan. Tull took his filled plate and walked away from the fire, walked straight toward where Buckner lay. He watched Tull coming and began to draw his knees up, ready to spring and run for it. Tull got to within a dozen paces of the bush and seated himself on a rock and began morosely eating.

Rigby, finishing with his food, walked to where a saddle lay and took a new rope from it. Fetching the rope, he came toward Tull and sat down on a rock close by. Neither man spoke. Tull continued eating; Rigby began playing the rope through his hands, working the newness from it.

Buckner tried not to breathe. He waited, having no choice. Presently Tull put his plate down on the grass and spoke, his voice stubborn and defensive. "All right, Spence. Go ahead and get it off your chest."

Rigby said in a level tone, "I already spoke my piece, Sam. Back there at the Brewster place when I told you you were a fool to go at Buckner when we had a bigger fish to fry. I thought when I pulled off the rest of the crew, you'd see the light. But you wanted blood. Suppose you'd killed him, Sam, and then had to kill the Lane girl besides. How would you have squared yourself with the law?"

"I'd have figured that out afterwards."

Rigby quit working the rope. "There might have been a way at that! I didn't think of it till now. The law might have thought it was Duke Jordan who planted lead in Ry Buckner. And that the girl just accidentally got in the way." He grew excited. "Now why didn't I see that this afternoon?"

"Because you've got nothing on your mind but putting a rope around Duke Jordan's neck, Spence." Tull turned his gaze full upon Rigby. "It's time we understand each other. You're set on using that rope. Maybe the reasons McQueen gave last night put the finger on why. Now don't go getting hot at me! He's the one who said you were a little man trying to look big. Your reasons don't mean a damn to me. Point is, I'm willing to string along. But if you've got a drive in you to hang Jordan, I've got a drive in me to put a bullet into Buckner. And I'm not pushing the point that you'd be smarter to let the law take care of Duke Jordan, because he really shouldn't matter to you anyway."

"What you're saying, then, is that if I've got a loco spot about Jordan, I should respect your hankering for Buckner's scalp?"

"Partners, Spence. That's the way it was supposed to be since the first of those secret little talks we started having about a year ago. And that brings up another thing. That partnership was to be down on paper—

signed, sealed, and delivered. No reason now why it can't be."

"The paper's drawn up, Sam. In my office. All it needs is signing, witnessing, and filing at the court-house. I'm thinking it might look better if Lark Rigby's grave were a bit older before that paper is filed."

"I don't agree," Tull said dispassionately. "If you're worried about town and range talk, nothing is going to look wrong. Lark died; you inherited; and you made me a partner. Your business has been saloons; mine has been cattle. A foremanship wasn't enough, so I held out for a partnership. That's why you drew up a paper, and as long as it's dated any time after last night, what's the difference?" His voice hardened. "You'd better take care of that, Spence. Maybe I've learned a few tricks from you about fancy scheming. I might just happen to have an ace in the hole."

Rigby stood up. He drew in the played-out rope and began coiling it. "All right, Sam. The paper will be signed and filed as soon as we get back to town." He glanced toward the fire and the crew loitering around it and lowered his voice. "We're in this thing together. You've got no worry, Sam."

"Maybe not," Tull said and stood up, too. "Some of the outfit is getting ready to bed down."

"I told them to, Sam. No sense stumbling around this mountain in the dark."

"I see it different," Tull said. "If Jordan does any riding, he's going to do it by night. I'm saddling up and having a look around."

"Uphill or down?"

"Down, I reckon."

"Back toward the Brewster place, Sam? It's still Buckner you're hunting, not Jordan."

"Looking for one, maybe I run into the other, Spence. And like I pointed out last night when you tried to line up Buckner against Jordan, if Buckner isn't on our side, he's against us."

"Sam," Rigby said, "you wanted a ranch of your own, and you've as good as got half of one right now. Think first of Hatchet when you make any play. Don't risk throwing away the whole game by some damned fool act just because you're packing a personal grudge. That's all I ask."

Tull said, "Just the same, I'm riding tonight."

"And I'm bedding down," Rigby said. "Come morning, I'll head the boys out in pairs in different directions. We'll comb this mountain fine. We can all join up here each sundown till we finish working this slope."

They both walked toward the fire. Buckner began crawling backwards. He got to the timber and eased through it to where he had left his horse. He stood beside the mount, thinking. This gulch was indeed to be Hatchet's base camp, but tomorrow the outfit would be spread thin. Should he wait for daylight and their departure, or should he try getting past the camp tonight, once they were asleep?

Debating, he heard a horse move along the trail through the timber, heading down toward the road at the end of the gulch. Sam Tull, going back to the Brewster place. He swung up into his own saddle.

Tull! Tull riding alone in search of Ry Buckner. Anger stirred in him again. He listened to the diminishing sounds of Tull's passage and knew what his own course would be, wise or not. He followed the trail out of the gulch, turned right onto the old road, and dropped downhill after Tull, keeping his mount to a walk.

Damn' foolish, this! Foolish to be heading away from the cave and what he hoped to learn there. Foolish to let an angry heart rule him, rather than a cool head, but there was this afternoon to remember, and Tull's stubborn determination to carry a grudge, and there was last night, too; and all this added up to his having business with Tull. You bet!

He stayed behind the man for a good three miles, wanting at least that much distance between them and Hatchet's camp. Often he had to gamble that Tull was holding to about the same pace as himself, for when he paused to listen for hoofbeats, he heard none. Needlefall and grass muffled the sound. When the moon came up, he saw the man below him in places where the road ran straight. Farther down and into the foothills, the country widened and the trees thinned out, and he had little trouble keeping Tull in sight.

Now the time had come to overtake the man. He lifted the borrowed gun from his holster and put spurs to his horse and came hard after Tull. As he closed the distance between them, he shouted, "Hatchet! Ho!"

Here lay the real gamble. Would Tull, who now heard the rider behind him, be thrown off guard for a moment? The shout was to make Tull think that the man on the backtrail was a Hatchet hand, sent after him by Spence Rigby. Tull swung his horse around, his hand dropping toward his gun. But he hesitated, undecided for a few seconds. Buckner came thundering upon him, gun in hand and shouting, "Up with 'em, Tull! Up, or I'll blow you out of that saddle!"

Recognition flared in Tull's eyes too late. The man's first astonishment gave way to a cold anger, his expression showing plainly his temptation to make a play in the face of that naked gun. Then he decided he'd better not. His hands went up. Buckner rode close to him and plucked the six-shooter from Tull's holster and tossed it aside.

"Get down, Tull," he said.

Tull dismounted and stood with his hands up, his face wooden in the moonlight. Buckner swung down from his own saddle and dropped the reins. He looked at Tull. He knew exactly why he had followed Tull and what he was going to do, and the blood pounded in his temples. He holstered his gun, unlatched his gunbelt and let it drop. He flung his hat aside and pulled off his coat.

"You made talk in the back room of the Frontier last night, Tull," he said. "I was to be worked over, with six men to do the job. Lumberjack style, you said. Fist and boot. This afternoon you had more to say. A yellow-bellied jailbird you called me. You wanted me to fight the way a man would. All right. I'm ready."

He took a step toward Tull, fists raised. Full understanding showed on Tull's face then, and this was the only time Buckner had ever seen a light of pure joy in the man's eyes. Tull lowered his arms and came at him swinging wildly. He parried that onslaught with his left arm and got under Tull's clumsy guard with his right fist in a meaty blow to the jaw. He put all his shoulder behind that blow. It lifted Tull from his feet and landed him hard on the back of his neck. He thought he had knocked Tull unconscious with that one lucky punch, but Tull rolled over and got dazedly to his hands and knees, shaking his head.

He hovered over Tull, glaring down at the man. He didn't want Tull conquered so easily. He wanted this to be a lasting fight with plenty of punishment handed out. "Get up!" he shouted. "Do you hear? You wanted a fight. Now stand up and do some fighting!"

But still Tull stayed on his hands and knees, groggy and befuddled. He took a step toward Tull. He was going to get the man by the collar and yank him to his feet. He reached for Tull, and suddenly the red rage lifted from his brain, and in that moment he knew exactly what had goaded him along Tull's trail and moved him to shuck his coat and come at Tull with fists swinging.

He had no love for Tull, but neither did he bear the man any real hate. Tull was what he was, brutal and ruthless, and Tull therefore did what his nature dictated. And Tull wanted him dead. You might hate a man for that, but unless you were of the man's own cut, you didn't answer brutality with brutality, and you didn't seize on names hurled and threats made as an excuse to come down to such a man's level.

No, the urge to batter Tull into insensibility had not possessed him because of Tull. He'd been angry, yes, but at someone else. He had vented on Tull the rage that had built in him ever since he had heard from Pru Lane about Dorcas's intended marriage.

Of course! Pru had realized what the news had done to him. "Even now your face looks different from when you rode here this afternoon," she'd said. "Older. Harder. I don't believe it was that round with Sam Tull that made it so."

He looked down at Tull now, anger fading out of him and shame taking its place; he looked at Tull with an odd sort of sorrow in him for this man who knew no way but the ruthless way.

Tull made one great effort to rise, then sank back to the ground, his arms outflung. The man lay there, groaning and cursing. Buckner walked back to where he had dropped his gunbelt. He buckled on the belt, picked up his coat and shrugged into it, and found his hat. He gathered up the reins and climbed onto his horse. He began to wheel the horse about to head back up the hill road.

Only instinct warned him. He turned in his saddle and saw Tull on hands and knees scuttling to where moonlight winked from his thrown six-shooter. He knew then that Tull had pretended to be worse hurt than he'd been, wanting, probably, a few more moments to gather his strength. He saw Tull grasp the gun and bring it up flaming. He tried reaching for his own gun too late. Something smote his left shoulder hard, the shock of that blow driving him into a daze. He reeled, sure that he was falling from the saddle; he clutched the horn.

He became dimly aware that his horse was running, and he bent all effort to one need. He must keep to the saddle while the night rushed by and a deeper darkness closed in, blinding him.

10 : Truce by Moonlight

He shook his head, trying to clear it. He kept himself conscious by sheer will. He had no strength to control the horse, and he sensed that the mount was heading downhill, carrying him back over the road toward the Brewster place. This was wrong, he knew. His business was on Table Mountain, at a certain cave. His business was with Duke. He had let himself be lured in the opposite direction because he had let anger rule him. This was the price he was paying, this ache of body, this woodenness of mind. Now he must let the horse run while he fought to stay in the saddle.

Was Tull still firing at him? How could he hear the blast of a six-shooter when there was a thunder in his head and a thunder of hoofs under him now that the road was no longer needle blanketed? Maybe Tull was mounted and hard after him. He had to keep ahead of Tull.

But he was going to fall. He knew it. Something had gone wrong with his sense of balance, and he jostled in the saddle, spineless, helpless. He had come into another of those mountain meadows. The moon was so bright it hurt his eyes, and the ancient road had become a silver ribbon that blurred and writhed and seemed to run every which direction.

He felt himself tipping. He commanded some last reserve of strength and hauled hard on the reins. He dropped the reins, ground-anchoring the horse. Falling to the left, he tried desperately to turn so that he would spare his wounded shoulder. As he hit the ground, pain stunned him, but still he held to the ragged edge of consciousness. He heard a clatter of hoofs. He tried to lift himself, tried to get at his gun, and this was sheer nightmare, this needing to move and not being able to. That would be Sam Tull come to finish the job, and he was helpless against Tull.

A horse and rider loomed up, closer and closer. He saw the rider dismount and run toward him. This wasn't Tull, not when the rider wore one of those divided skirts, and he shouted, "Pru—!" but the name was only an explosion of sound within his brain and nothing that hit the ear. He saw the face that hovered over him, a face that swam like a reflection in water, and his brain shouted again, another name, the right name, "Dorcas—!" Then somebody tossed a blanket over the moon, blotting it out . . .

He opened his eyes to find the moon back again, fiercer than before. He threw his right arm over his face and said, "Somebody blow that damn' thing out!" Then his brain cleared. He lay flat on his back, with Dorcas crouched beside him. Her horse stood a dozen paces away, reins trailing, and his own was just beyond it. He tried to sit up, and his left shoulder was a stone that had to be lifted, but he managed. "How long have I been out?" he asked.

"Not more than ten minutes," Dorcas said. "There's blood on your coat. I couldn't do much with you unconscious. Let's have a look at your shoulder."

He began working out of his coat, and she helped him. It struck him then how queer this meeting was. Not the fact that she happened to be here in the foothills by night—that was understandable, considering that she, too, had been searching for Duke—but how queer that the first words between them had been the ones spoken. In prison, after her last letter, he had sometimes wondered if they would come face to face again and what they would say to each other when that happened. He had even rehearsed speeches, pruning out words and rearranging the ones left; but they hadn't been tonight's words.

He got his coat off and unbuttoned his shirt and carefully pulled the cloth from the wound. He tried peering at the wound, but it was difficult to see, and he touched it gingerly with his fingertips. The bullet had torn a bad gash where his upper left arm joined to his shoulder, but the lead had apparently passed on. Shock and loss of blood had undone him.

Dorcas peered, too. "You'll need a pad and tie," she said. She stood up and walked a few paces, putting her back to him. "Look the other way, Ry," she said.

He did, and he heard cloth tear, and he guessed that she was ripping strips from an undergarment. She came back and fitted a folded square of cloth against the wound and tied it in place with a long strip which she knotted under his armpit. He studied her face as she worked. Older, of course, but just as beautiful, and yet there was a difference. A more determined face—the set features of one who knew what she wanted and was going to have it. He remembered last night at the court-house corner and his urge to call after her, and he wondered now if any call of his could ever reach to her.

She stood up, her work finished. "All right, Ry," she said. "Let's have it now. You ran into somebody's gun. Duke's?"

"Sam Tull's," he said. "A couple of miles above here. He's probably on my trail."

"Somebody's coming now," she said, and he had to admire the way she kept her voice so calm.

He saw a man riding hard across the meadow toward them. The reassuring factor was that the man came not down the road but out of the west, across country. Still, he struggled to his feet and drew his gun and held it ready, his real fear for Dorcas, caught here with him. Seemed he was constantly bad luck to the Lane sisters. Then he recognized the gnarled body of the rider even before the man reached them and swung down from the saddle and he could make out Gulley Jordan's heavy-beaked face. Gulley shouted, "Duke! I saw you there on the ground! You hurt, boy?"

Buckner put his gun away. "Look closer, Gulley," he said. "Right build—wrong man. Hatchet made the same mistake at the Signal depot last night."

Gulley said, "Riley Buckner, by God!" Whether he was astonished or angry, it was difficult to tell. He looked at Dorcas, hostility in his eyes.

"I rather guessed it was you following me," she said. "Now you've caught up."

"Girl, I thought you'd lead me to Duke," Gulley snapped. "I didn't figure it was Ry Buckner you were hunting. Ain't you made up your mind yet which man is your man?"

Dorcas sighed wearily. "I just happened to hit here as he came riding down the road and fell off his horse. Sam Tull used a gun on him."

Gulley frowned, looking at Buckner again. "You wounded, boy? You'd better be got to town, to a doctor." He said this grudgingly.

Buckner said stiffly, "I'll make out."

"Till you tumble from that saddle again," Gulley muttered. "I wouldn't leave a hurt dog alone in these hills." He turned to Dorcas. "Somebody's got to see he makes town. After all, he was a Boxed J hand once."

Buckner grew angry. "I never asked anything from you but a day's pay for a day's work. This dog will lick his own wounds." He walked to his horse and swung himself to the saddle, but his head reeled, and he swayed.

He heard Gulley say to Dorcas, "You can see he ain't likely to make it alone." There was some sort of appeal in that comment, and Buckner could sense the hesitancy in Dorcas's attitude. Much here he didn't understand, but it was plain that Dorcas had been on her way to make contact with Duke and Gulley had been following her, hoping thus to be led to Duke; and now Gulley found himself in a quandary. If he turned toward town without Dorcas, he lost his chance.

None of which set well with himself, Buckner decided.. Whatever he might have wanted from either of them he had wanted in court five years ago or in the prison loneliness afterwards. His own need now lay back in the hills, but he questioned whether he could reach the cave tonight with his shoulder hurting this way. In any case, there was that bandage on his wound, and so there was a debt to Dorcas, and thus he had to warn her.

"Dorcas," he called, and she looked up at him. "If it's the cave where you expect to find Duke, you'd better know that Hatchet is camped in Timmerman Gulch. You'll never get past them tonight."

"The cave!" Gulley said, understanding. "I never thought of the cave!" He appealed to Dorcas. "Girl, don't go trying any damn' fool thing that will lead Spence Rigby straight to Duke. You come along now with us."

She had that wilful look, Buckner saw. Likely she would pay no heed to his warning nor to Gulley's. But she also looked thoughtful, as though she were taking all things into consideration. Plainly she wished to elude Gulley, and probably if she chose now to go on into the hills, Gulley would follow her, Duke being more important to him than Riley Buckner could ever be. And here he sat, teetering in the saddle, not wanting their help but knowing that he needed it.

Dorcas walked to her horse and mounted. "Dad Jordan is right," she said. "We can't leave you alone. Not wounded and with Sam Tull perhaps hunting you."

"Dorcas," he said sharply, "I reckon your place is with Duke. I didn't tell you about Hatchet to stop you, but only to keep you out of trouble." He raised his hand toward his bandaged shoulder. "I had to do that much at least."

She moved her horse up stirrup to stirrup with his. "Maybe I owe you something, too, Ry," she said. "Let's ride."

Gulley grunted, climbed to his saddle and brought his horse up to flank Buckner's. With Gulley on one side of him and Dorcas on the other, they headed on down the road. Buckner felt caught up in a sort of moon madness, for this was an odd situation indeed, to be riding with these two, the three of them allies and enemies at the same time. The real allegiance of Dorcas and Gulley belonged to Duke in the long run, he knew, and their going with him was a sort of truce come of necessity.

No denying that he was glad for their presence, though. He had said he could make out alone, but he knew better. The smash of that forty-five slug had taken too much out of him, that and the loss of blood; and dizziness swept him at times, and he had to grasp the saddlehorn. Once when he tipped far to the left, Gulley had to reach out and steady him. They seemed to have been riding forever when they dropped down to the Brewster place, and here Gulley asked, "How you feelin'?"

"Fine," Buckner said, but it wasn't so.

They had all three pulled to a stop. Before them the ruined buildings reared, silent, ghostly, deserted. No covered wagon in the yard now, no Reverend Jones and son, no Billy Larb, no Pru. Gulley made the decision. "We stop here and rest a mite."

Dorcas swung down from her saddle, and Buckner

dismounted, too. He staggered with his first steps, and Dorcas looked at him worriedly. Gulley said, frowning, "Maybe we'd better finish out the night here. Go on inside, you two. I'll put the horses in the barn. No use showin' sign we're here if Tull should come snoopin'."

Buckner walked to the rotted porch and through the doorway that had been so hard gained that afternoon. Dorcas brushed close to him. Moonlight shafted through a window, and on the floor lay a folded square of paper held down by a rock. Dorcas picked up the paper, opened it, and moved closer to a window in order to read.

"From Pru?" Buckner asked.

"Now how would you know that?"

"I found her here this afternoon, Dorcas. She was waiting for you and a preacher and a second witness to a marriage."

She put the note in her pocket, and when she turned toward him her face was in shadow, but her voice was as he remembered it from other days, soft and appealing. "Ry, I know you must hate me," she said. "Will you try to understand that I'm doing what I have to do?"

He shook his head. "I don't hate you, Dorcas. I could never hate you." He wanted to say more, to tell her what troubled him and how he had to see Duke and get the answer and how the whole thing was the more mixed up now because he had learned she was marrying Duke. He fumbled for the words, but the heavy step of Gulley Jordan sounded on the porch, and the old man came in carrying an armload of saddle blankets and his own saddle.

"Best we bed down," he said.

"I'll take the outdoors to this smelly place," Buckner said.

"Not with frost on the grass come morning and you with a wounded shoulder," Gulley growled. He started out again.

"You can fetch the extra blankets I was taking to Duke," Dorcas said. "He isn't going to get them tonight. Wait, I'll lend you a hand."

They both came back bringing the rest of the blankets and the other two saddles. Buckner carried his own saddle and blanket to another room. He spread the blanket on the floor and put the saddle in position for a pillow and sat down and tugged off his boots. He shouldn't be here, he told himself. He should be back in the hills, making his search. But what he wanted more than anything else in the world at this moment was to sleep. He felt he could sleep for a million years.

Gulley brought his saddle and blanket to this same room. Buckner could make out his movements dimly as Gulley prepared a bed. Buckner took off his gun-belt and laid it nearby and eased into the blanket. He could hear a stirring elsewhere in the house—Dorcas preparing for sleep. He settled down, favoring his wounded shoulder. Gulley seemed to be settling down, too.

"Ry—?" Gulley called then.

"Yes—?" sleepily.

"I loaded a gun this morning. One of those bullets was maybe for you. I'm hopin' not. I'll ask out plain so we'll know how we stand with each other. You huntin' my boy?"

"Yes, Gulley."

"To kill him?"

"I've got to talk to him, Gulley."

The old man held silent for a long time. "Ry," he said then, "I'm going to ask another question. Five years ago, when you started home from Jupiter City with that carpetbag with the cattle sale money, did you look into the bag to see how much cash it held?"

He shook the cobwebs of drowsiness away. "No, I didn't."

"Then you really couldn't have sworn that the bag held money?"

He was fully awake now. "What are you getting at?"

Another long silence. Then: "Ry, I went to Jupiter City myself on some business that same fall, after your trial. I heard remarks dropped here and there. I started doin' a little snoopin' then. Once that herd was paid for and the rest of the crew headed home, you and Duke hung around the saloons and gamblin' places. That come out at the trial. What didn't come out was that Duke did some heavy gambling. I found out quite a bit about some big losses. I didn't hear of no big winnings, though."

Buckner rolled over. "Just why in hell are you telling *me* this?" He looked toward Gulley and made out that the old man had propped himself on an elbow and was staring at him.

"I ain't a soft man," Gulley said. "Reckon I just never was able to afford being a soft man. But I've always tried to be just. If I ever had a blind spot, it was Duke. I closed you out of my mind five years ago, because I kind of guessed even then that if I started thinkin' in your favor, I might end up thinkin' things about Duke I didn't want to think. But last night I come out of sleep callin' your name; and tonight when I come on you wounded, I knew I owed you something and no denyin' it. Damn it, man, this ain't easy to say!"

"I'm listening, Gulley."

"What I'm trying to get across is that maybe I made a wrong judgment about you five years ago, and maybe I'm throwin' myself on your mercy by tellin' you this, hopin' that I'll get some mercy from you for Duke. Let's just assume that he's the one should have gone to the pen, not you. Mind you, I'm not saying that's so! But wouldn't it be punishment enough that he's runnin' from a murder charge now? Couldn't you go easy on him if you catch up with him? Even if the truth should be that he got himself in a terrible tight five years ago and had to pile one wrong on top of another because he couldn't see no other way out?"

"What I want, Gulley, is to hear what Duke's got to say to *me* about all that."

"And then—?"

"I'll take it from there."

Gulley's voice turned harsh. "Then understand this: if you're his enemy, you're my enemy, boy, and there's still that shell I'm packin' with your name on it. I risked tellin' you what I learned in Jupiter City in the hope you'd see it my way."

Just the same, Buckner thought, *what you've told me is that you suspect Duke gambled that money away in Jupiter on nights he slipped away from me and then sent me home with a worthless carpetbag, then stole it from me on the trail so his shortage wouldn't be discovered. And this is supposed to wring mercy from me!* But suddenly he saw behind the bluster of Gulley Jordan and so saw him

revealed as a frightened old man, crying out in his loneliness, needing help and hoping to find it in, of all men,
Riley Buckner. A just man, Gulley, with that one admitted blind spot.

It all made a great deal to think about, but he was too
tired, too hard used to keep his mind on it now. He
wanted to talk more with Gulley, but in spite of himself
he slept. . . .

He awoke to gray dawn and that feeling of strange-
ness that comes with awakening in a strange place. He
awoke to find Dorcas bending above him, removing a
blanket from him, and only when he saw the blanket
did he realize that she must have come in here after
he'd slept and put one of the extra blankets over him.
One of Duke's blankets. He would have cried out her
name, but she put a finger to her lips, cautioning silence. She nodded in the direction of Gulley, who lay
snoring.

"How are you feeling?" she whispered.

He sat up. His shoulder was mighty stiff and ached
dully, but he felt refreshed, able to cope with things.
"Fine," he said.

"Can you make it to town by yourself?"

"I'm not going to town," he said. "A night's sleep was
all I needed."

"Ry," she said, "I've saddled, and I'm going to ride
now. I was tempted to slip away from here in the middle of the night, but I decided I had to wait to see how
you were, whether you needed more help. You don't, so
I'll be on my way."

"Because of that note Pru left here for you?"

She hesitated. "Yes, Ry. She wrote me that Reverend Jones couldn't wait here and said where I might find him and her today."

"I'll be riding, too," he said.

She looked toward Gulley. "It would be too much to ask of you," she said, "to keep him from my trail."

"Girl," he said, "don't you understand that he's as much on Duke's side as you are?"

"Except that I don't think he'd want me to meet Duke for the reason I'll be meeting him."

"You mean he wouldn't take to the notion of the marriage, I suppose."

"I'm trying to be fair, Ry. I could have turned his horse and yours astray, but I didn't. You can have the rest of your sleep without worrying over that. We'll all start about even from where we met last night."

"Except that I'll be wearing a bandage you put on me."

"Bought and paid for long ago," she said. "It needn't count one way or the other."

He nodded. A truce by moonlight dispelled in the grayness of dawn. A trio who had ridden together now to go their separate ways. A game played according to the code of each of them. Fair enough.

He wanted to say, "Good luck, girl," but he couldn't, now that they were going to be at cross purposes again. He watched her slip from the room. Old Gulley still snored. Presently he heard Dorcas walk her horse from the yard. He knew that he must be up and doing. Hatchet would be prowling the hills, and he still had to get to Duke first.

11 : The Sleepless Ones

Spence Rigby, watching Sam Tull saddle up and ride from Hatchet's camp in Timmerman Gulch, had stood troubled and thoughtful after the timber had swallowed the man. Damned if he liked Tull's attitude. Partners, Tull had said in that little talk they'd just had, but what he really remembered was Tull's getting mouthy about his wanting to put a rope around Duke Jordan's neck. And bringing up what McQueen had said last night at the courthouse about the why of that. Rubbing it in! As good as saying McQueen had figured it right that since everybody tallied Spencer Rigby as pretty small, he had to hang a man to prove how wide his britches really were.

He spat. How the devil could anybody know his real reason for wanting Duke Jordan dead when he hadn't stopped to put a name to it himself? Only thing clear was that since last night he'd known he wouldn't rest till he saw Duke dangling, and lynching was quicker than lawful hanging. Hangtree fever, eh? Well, he had a cure for it!

But the person bothering him now was Sam Tull himself. Duke would have to keep until tomorrow when there was daylight for hunting him. Sam Tull was another matter, getting proddy about that partnership paper not being filed and hinting at an ace in the hole.

A bluff that last, likely, but the trouble with Tull was that he could get himself in deep and drag Hatchet along with him. Consider that fool play at the Brewster place this afternoon, for instance. Talk yourself blue in the face, yet there was no budging the man. True, he had seen a way afterwards to have got Tull off the hook he might have fastened himself onto, but that hadn't meant anything to Tull. "I've got a drive in me to put a bullet into Buckner," Tull had insisted, and that was Tull summing himself up. A man of direct and violent action. A man who needed constant watching. A fine partner to have in a chancy game not yet finished!

No, he couldn't just let Tull go riding off through the night, set on the notion of finding Riley Buckner and having it out. Not with Tull the kind to act first and think afterwards. He turned to Abe Lofstrum, who was fixing a bed. "Saddle up for me, Abe," he said. Lofstrum showed surprise. "Get at it, man!" Rigby snapped, and Abe moved to obey.

Big Rufe York sat cross-legged by the dying fire, smoking a last cigarette. Rigby walked to him and nodded in the direction Tull had taken. "I'm going for a little ride, Rufe. You'll be in charge till I get back."

York grunted, his face impassive. Rigby stood waiting till Lofstrum led up his saddled horse. He mounted and lifted a hand. Rufe and Abe nodded. Other Hatchet riders were busy with their own doings, some preparing beds, some already rolled into blankets. No one spoke as he rode away. It seemed to Rigby that their silence was a sneer.

A wild foreman ahead—a contemptuous crew behind. That was the kind of outfit *he'd* got! Well, they would learn to respect him, given time. Last night they had come to town on the heels of the news of the shooting, all except a few like Lofstrum who had been posted by Tull to guard the trails Duke Jordan might have taken. They had watched the depot against the chance that Duke might try to board the freight, and they had massed at the Frontier and been impatient to hit the saddle in pursuit of Duke. They had accepted the fact that Spence Rigby now rodded Hatchet, and they had been with him to a man this morning. But through the long day he had learned what their allegiance really amounted to: habit, the hired hand's loyalty to the iron for which he rode. He was not Lark Rigby to them, and he never would be.

Now why was it that men had looked with respect at Lark but not at him? Lark had been no man with the ready smile, the winning way. Lark had been tough and forthright; but even Sam Tull, who had openly hated Lark, had stayed in line when he rode at Lark's command.

Yes, Lark had always been the Rigby who counted. Lark, seven years his senior and twenty feet taller among men. Lark, who had started a two-bit spread and built it big, working hard in the years when Spence Rigby had been drifting from town to town, saloon owner sometimes, gambler sometimes, putting behind him a parade of places—Deadwood, Cheyenne, Miles

City—a parade of failures. For no matter how firm a foothold he gained, his establishment always became the one shunned, until at last he had come to Signal, to Lark's own stamping grounds, and even Lark had turned his face from him because of the reputation the Frontier soon got.

Watered whiskey, they said, and rigged games. Hell, a man had to give himself some edge! Shouldn't it count for something that he cast warmth while Lark had been cold as stone? Sure, he'd sometimes made promises he couldn't keep, swung deals that wouldn't stand the test of light, forgotten friends who needed remembering. What man hadn't? But the upshot was that Lark had had everybody's respect, and Lark's crew now backed him only because the man hunted had used a gun on Lark.

Thinking this, he made the right-hand turn from the gulch onto the old road and dropped downhill, knowing that Tull would be heading back to the Brewster place. He rode slowly, a fretful man. How much could he count on Hatchet if he did corner Duke Jordan? "Men easy twisted when the time comes," McQueen had said last night. That was the string to pluck. Remind them of what had happened to Lark, once they had Duke in their hands.

Then, in a stretch where the road dropped straight before him, he saw a rider ahead. Tull? He couldn't be sure, so he drifted slowly behind the man. First moonlight, dappled by tree branches, touched the fellow, and for an instant he had a full glimpse. Not tall enough or lean enough to be Tull. Duke Jordan? Rigby's pulse leaped. Still he wasn't sure. He kept drifting downward to foothill country, and with the more open vista he knew he had been mistaken a second time. The rider ahead was pretty much of Duke's build, but he was Riley Buckner.

Just what was Buckner up to? Why was he heading downhill at this time? Tull must be farther below. Was Buckner following Tull? No telling, but before a good gambler took cards, he first figured the game being played. He continued trailing Buckner, keeping a safe distance between them; and when the country spread broader, he saw still another horseman even farther ahead. That had to be Tull.

In a few minutes Buckner began galloping, taking up the slack between himself and Tull, and Buckner's cry, "Hatchet! Ho!" lifted to Rigby. He checked his horse and bent forward in the saddle, peering hard, and plain in the moonlight he saw Tull swing his horse around and Buckner come up with him. Buckner's second shout, "Up with 'em, Tull! Up, or I'll blow you out of that saddle!" came clear.

Now was the moment to spur forward and give Buckner the surprise Tull had just got, but still Rigby held his horse in check. *See it through!* instinct whispered. Buckner had crowded close to Tull; Rigby guessed that Tull was being disarmed. Buckner said something, but the words did not carry. Tull climbed from his horse, and Buckner dismounted, too. Buckner seemed to be getting out of his coat, talking the while, and then Tull came at him with arms swinging wildly. Buckner struck, and Tull went down.

Buckner hovered over Tull. Again Buckner shouted, something about wanting Tull to get up and fight. But

Tull wasn't getting up, and Buckner merely stood for a while and then walked away and picked up something —his gunbelt, probably—and got into his coat and climbed onto his horse. And Tull, on his hands and knees, was suddenly bringing up a flaming gun. Buckner's horse bolted, heading downhill.

Tull got to his feet, flourishing the gun. He took a staggering step or two and almost fell. He looked after Buckner and raised the gun, but Buckner was already out of range.

Rigby jogged his horse now and rode on downward. He saw Tull look up at his coming, and he raised his free hand and shouted, "Sam, it's me! I got worried about you and followed." He came to within a dozen feet of Tull. "I saw the last of it, Sam. Too bad I didn't get here sooner."

Tull didn't bother to reply. His face was stone, except for the eyes, where hate dwelt. He glared in the direction Buckner had gone. He cased his gun, lurched to his horse, gathered up the reins, and set a foot in the left stirrup. He had his back to Rigby, and in Rigby there was no conscious prompting. He brought out his own gun and shot Tull between the shoulder blades.

Tull went down in a tangle of arms and legs but free of the stirrup. His horse bolted a few paces, then stood trembling. Rigby looked down at Tull dead and sprawling, the moonlight full on that skull face. No, he had not known he was going to shoot Tull until the gun had come into his hand, yet he faced the fact that some such intent had been in the back of his mind from the time he'd decided to take Tull's trail. What he hadn't expected was such an opportunity as this. Tull dead, with

Duke Jordan or Riley Buckner to get the blame, for who else in these hills tonight would have any known reason to kill the man?

Tull dead, and a partnership dissolved. Tull dead, and the secret between them dead, too, and only one last thing needing doing, the big thing. Never mind that now; he had things to attend to here. He would take the bridle off Tull's horse and let the animal stray where it pleased. And he would make some small pretense of hiding the body, which was what Buckner or Jordan might likely do under the circumstances. He would hide it, but not too well. He would proceed immediately to this tidying-up.

The last big thing must wait till tomorrow, when he would take Duke Jordan's trail again.

The grass-filled tick rustled beneath him as Virgil McQueen rolled over upon that makeshift mattress and tried to sleep. Must be an hour now since he had bedded down. Darkness lay thick in the Pothook bunkhouse, and he could hear the snoring of many men. The thought kept crowding him that he should be up in the hills hunting Duke Jordan. Maybe he should get up right now and lay a rope on his horse, pastured with Pothook's saddle stock, and get to riding. Better that than tossing about, wondering what good could come of that talk he'd had with Dorcas Lane this afternoon.

Talk! He'd grown sick of talk! There had been plenty of it when he had stopped at Pothook near sundown, eaten with the crew, played poker here in the bunkhouse, and been asked to stay the night if he chose. Idle talk, pointless talk. Talk of how poor beef prices had been since '87 and no sign of an upturn, talk of how many grangers were moving into the state—a couple thousand of them in 1880, somebody had said; near six thousand of them now. Talk of that Johnson County War down in Wyoming last spring; and resentful talk of how Congress had authorized President Harrison to set aside parts of the public domain as national forests, shutting off good summer graze. The betting was that Grover Cleveland would defeat Harrison in the election coming up soon.

He had listened with only half an ear. No worry of his who got to be president. His concern would be the county's choice for sheriff come November eighth. His opponent was a hayshaker whose candidacy would have been a joke a couple of terms back. Beat the man and he'd be done with worry, likely. The wild, violent West was passing even now—that Johnson County fracas had been a last whoop and holler—and sheriffing could shortly be an old man's job. But what about here and now? What about bringing in Duke Jordan, outlawed killer?

There'd been talk this evening about Duke, too; and though no Pothook hand had come straight out with a question, he had seen puzzlement on many a face, plain as if he'd been asked why he was roundsiding in a bunkhouse while Duke had to be caught. They'd given the edge to Duke in their talk, liking Duke some better than they'd liked Lark Rigby. Just the same, these Pothook hands cast votes, and that gave them the right to wonder why their sheriff wasn't about his business.

He'd hinted that he was awaiting a development. A

few years ago he wouldn't have bothered, safe in the knowledge that his reputation answered all questions, asked and unasked. But likely they were thinking what others had been whispering, that he was getting too old. And it was true, damn it! Too old to draw a gun with real speed. Too old to risk wearing his gun last night when he'd admitted Spence Rigby to his office. Ry Buckner, coming to his rescue, had guessed why he'd shucked his gun-belt. Hell, he'd as good as told Ry why he'd tried to blackmail him into helping catch Duke. If he could only get Duke into jail, there might be an end to this trouble and no more call for a gun and no black mark against him at election time.

Again he stirred on the tick. One accomplishment today. He'd made Dorcas Lane see that it would be to her advantage to persuade Duke to surrender. The girl wanted her man as well as his money. He'd admired the way she'd owned up to her ambitions. An honest girl, Dorcas, in her own calculating way. But she was the one with good practical sense, not Duke: so the question was whether she could argue Duke into giving himself up. Well, he'd know by four o'clock tomorrow afternoon, and that couldn't be more than sixteen hours from now.

But still he fretted, feeling that he should be up and riding; and come to think about it, he could and would, come morning. His pledged word put no barrier against that. All he'd promised was that he wouldn't follow Dorcas. Nothing wrong, though, with his getting into the hills and sniffing for sign against the possibility of Dorcas failing in her persuasion. Nothing lost if he did a little poking around first and then rode to town tomorrow night and found Duke and Dorcas sitting in his office awaiting him.

Where to start? He lay thinking of Table Mountain and all the lesser Garnets; and even Table could be a month's work, with its mighty slopes, its benches, its gulches. Now where would Duke likely be holed up?

He thought of Duke the man and of Duke the boy, working backward in mind across all the years he had known Duke. He had to chuckle, remembering that unlatched basement window in the courthouse and how it had stayed unlatched. Quite a pair of young scamps, Duke and Ry Buckner. Not mean, not vicious, just wild, with the wildness multiplied by their being paired. Real Injun blood brothers.

Now what had made him think of that? Something old Doc Fargo had said years back? He struggled to remember exactly what Doc had told him. "Cut themselves with a jackknife, the young fools. Of course they didn't much more than scratch themselves, Sheriff, but they could have got into real trouble. Might have bled to death, miles from town, up there in a cave at the head of Timmerman. They were looking pretty peaked and scared when they got here to me."

"A cave up Timmerman?" he'd said. "I don't seem to recollect such, Doc."

"It's pretty much out of the way, Sheriff. I gather those kids found it a few summers ago and play there regularly."

That was how the talk had run. And now, these years later in Pothook's bunkhouse, he nearly sat bolt upright in his excitement. That cave! He'd never had a look at it; there'd been no reason. A place Duke Jordan had known as a boy. A place Duke might have remembered now that he'd turned fugitive.

Should he pile out of this bunk and start riding tonight? The cave could be worth looking into. But it wouldn't make much sense to go prowling the darkness, and he reckoned he could use some rest first. That, too, was part of turning old, the need to ease old muscles and store up strength for the real calls on it. The cave could wait; it would be there tomorrow. He had to sleep, and he tried willing himself to sleep, but excitement still held him. At last he drifted away.

Somewhere in the great distances beyond the bunkhouse a coyote mourned the moon.

Thank heavens it was a still night, Prudence thought, with no wind hammering the house as it had last night. She snuggled deeper in her bed. A wind would be too much for her taut nerves after all the day had held. But now there was such a silence that she could hear her mother turn in bed in the next room. She hoped Maw had gone to sleep and so was done with talking.

She had awaited Dorcas at the Brewster place till nearly dark and then had had the long ride back to Signal. She had found her mother querulous and concerned, with most of her concern centered on Dorcas. She had had to listen while Maw cooked her a late supper, talking ceaselessly the while. At the mercantile all day Maw had listened to what the town thought and speculated. A hundred rumors were running wild, it seemed, what with Lark Rigby dead and Duke a fugitive and Oliver Landers telling the story of Dorcas's coming late last night to buy a marriage license.

"No, Maw," she had said wearily, "I didn't see Dorcas," and, "Yes, Maw, it was word from Dorcas that Billy Larb fetched, but Dorcas wasn't where I expected to find her." And then, with the questions growing more pointed: "I'm sorry, Maw, but I simply can't tell you what's up. It's Dorcas's secret, not mine. You'll have to wait till you can talk to her."

She had told her mother that she would be riding again tomorrow, starting early. What she hadn't told was that she had left a note at Brewsters' as good as promising Dorcas she'd be standing by again. She'd carefully worded the note so it would make little sense to anyone but Dorcas, yet she'd managed to explain that Reverend Jones had moved on to a certain west-end ranch, and that she, Pru, would go to that ranch, too, so Dorcas could find them both there if she wanted to keep the rendezvous tomorrow that had failed today. If Dorcas found the note, she could read between the lines and know where to bring Duke for the marriage.

Her mother called from the other room. "Prudence? You awake?"

Wearily: "Yes, Maw."

"If you see Dorcas tomorrow, you tell her I just hope she's doing the right thing. People kept making insinuations today. Martha Castner said right out that Dorcas certainly hadn't been in any hurry before and it didn't look proper for her to be buying a marriage license with Duke on the run. Nasty old woman! She said it was pretty plain Dorcas wanted to be sure she got to be Mrs. Jordan before the law hanged Duke."

Yes, Prudence thought, *and that's just about the size of it!*

"I let her know *some* people would consider it very loyal of Dorcas to be willing to marry Duke and him in so much trouble. *Some* girls—and I didn't mention her Gertrude that quit Bob Garber when he got drunk that time—would be running the opposite direction once their man really needed them!"

"Go to sleep, Maw," Pru said. "Don't fret about it. Dorcas knows what she's doing."

And that was gospel, you could bet. Dorcas had always known what she was doing. Hark back to Dorcas six and herself four, the two of them half-orphaned, and even then Dorcas had fought for security. Dorcas the precocious one, mature in pigtails. Dorcas, who had sometimes seemed more mother to a kid sister than Maw Lane herself, too busy with the struggle for existence to have time for much else.

Thinking this, she was softened by a host of memories, and she knew that she loved them both, for they had shared adversity and been bound closer by it. She was sorry then for being impatient with her mother and for thinking the same things about Dorcas that some of the townspeople were now thinking. Any memories of Dorcas held the myriad kindnesses of Dorcas. The difference between them always had been that Dorcas had seen poverty as a grim foe, while she, Prudence, had seen it as an adventure, romantic as books.

Well, they were big girls now, marriageable girls, and Dorcas was set on marrying. Let all the furies be hunting Duke Jordan, and Pru knew Dorcas would somehow contrive to bring Duke before a preacher. No point in worrying about Dorcas, and it wasn't Dorcas who was on her mind, really, nor had been since last night.

She looked toward the window, outlined dimly by first moonlight. She remembered Ry Buckner coming through that window; and she chuckled, thinking how Ry had been sure he'd scared her to death. But the chuckle died with the thought of her second meeting, today's meeting, with Ry. She had told him about Dorcas and Duke and seen him change. She had done that to him, then watched him ride away. To where? It was no destination in space that concerned her but the place he might reach in mood, some savage shore of no return.

But why let this worry her? He had broad shoulders; she had told him so. What did he mean to her, really? She remembered him from five years before, a big, genial, shy fellow coming to this very house to court Dorcas, clumsy at love-making but good to see. She had liked him and felt a certain kinship—he had known poverty, too, and seen it as an adventure put behind once he'd reached manhood. Certainly she wasn't in love with him. It was just that he was someone caught up in Dorcas's life and then discarded because he hadn't fitted into Dorcas's ambitions. Was it her job to go around picking up the pieces strewn behind Dorcas?

Crazy thinking, this. She had better get to sleep. Morning came early, and it was a far piece to the west end of the valley. But as she began dozing off, she was struck by one more thought, though she was far too sleepy to pursue it. She only knew she was glad it was Duke whom Dorcas intended marrying, not Ry.

12 : To the Cave

Frost lay on the grass, sparkling in first sunlight, when Riley Buckner came out of the Brewster place toting his saddle and blanket and strode toward the barn. In the house, Gulley Jordan still slept. Gulley knew about the cave now, for to warn Dorcas about Timmerman Gulch last night had meant speaking before Gulley, considering. Gulley would be riding, too. But there was this little edge of time to be put to advantage.

Five minutes later he headed up the hill road, breakfasting in the saddle from the last of the restaurant food he'd fetched. Have to tighten his belt from here on out. His shoulder still felt heavy; and when he'd finished eating, he shifted the reins to his right hand and worked his left arm piston-fashion, limbering it. When he came near a little creek, a mile or two above Brewster's he cut over to it, stripped off coat and shirt, and removed the pad from his shoulder. The gash had quit bleeding, and he carefully washed the wound. He tried fastening the pad back in place, but it was such an awkward business that he gave it up. No time to waste.

He stood listening for hoofs on the backtrail, and even though the silence of the hills held, he guessed that Gulley would be riding by now.

Somewhere ahead was Dorcas, her sign plain and fresh from the house they had quit.

He hit the road again. A few more miles of climbing and he sensed he was nearing the spot where he had overtaken Sam Tull last night. He wondered if Tull prowled in search of him or had gone back to Hatchet's camp. Soon he reached the place where they had had their one-blow fight. He could see where they had trampled down the grass. The sun had lifted high enough now so that frost no longer glinted, but there was blood on the grass. This brought him to an abrupt halt. Blood? There had been no blood shed but his own when the bullet had struck him.

Puzzled and excited, he bent forward, studying the grass. Now he could see where some heavy object had been dragged, possibly at the end of a saddle rope, leaving a path of flattened grass and a thin trail of blood. He veered from the road and walked the horse along this pathway, walked it to a clump of trees a hundred yards away. And here he found the sprawled body of Sam Tull, face down, with a bullet hole between the shoulder blades.

He dismounted and crouched beside the body, studying it. How the devil did Tull come to be here finished off in such a fashion? He remembered how he had left Tull last night and climbed on his horse, only to find Tull scuttling on hands and knees for his thrown gun. When Tull had brought that gun up flaming, he'd tried to get at his own gun, but he was sure he hadn't made it. He'd been lost then in a nightmare of pain and shock aboard a bolting horse, and it had been someone else who'd shot Tull and then dragged his body here.

Duke? Duke riding by night and come upon an enemy? But Duke was no back-shooter, give him that.

He shook his head and mounted his horse again. He didn't like leaving Tull lying here, but he had no tool with which to bury him and no time to take the body to town. He got back to the road and followed it upward again and was soon to where it became a winding lane flanked on either side by crowding timber. He rode slowly, carefully, not certain of what might lie beyond each bend. His caution soon served him. He heard voices, sharp in the mountain air, and he pulled his horse off into timber and waited till two riders dropped down the road past him. He had only a glimpse of them, but he recognized the Darby brothers riding single file.

Hatchet on the hunt. He remembered lying outside their camp last night and Spence Rigby saying, "Come morning, I'll head the boys out in pairs in different directions," and he waited now in concealment, debating. Hit the road again and he was apt to find Timmerman Gulch deserted, with Rigby's crew flung out upon the trails; but by the same token, he might find Hatchet hands around any turn. He looked at the thicket behind him, a density of lodgepole pine and spruce, deadfall and underbrush, impenetrable at first glance but safe from searchers, perhaps, by that very token. He looked and made his choice.

He began working through this back country and soon had to dismount and lead his horse. The sun climbed higher, and he sweated, and after a while thirst became a torment, and each mile gained was sheer toil. Again and again he had to backtrack and go round-about, finding himself blocked by tangles of fallen timber, but always he kept veering east, and by noon he looked from the rim down into Timmerman Gulch. He judged he was above the place where Hatchet had camped and he might safely descend into the gulch now, but there was no way off this rocky crest. Not at this point. He could have made it by abandoning the horse, but he struggled on, leading the mount and following the rim of the gulch.

An hour later he came to a break in the sheer face of the cliff, for here the rim had crumbled away and a shale slope spread downward. He ventured the slope carefully, hauling the reluctant horse behind him. They came slipping and sliding, sending a small avalanche ahead; and before they reached bottom, the attempt seemed folly, and he regretted the try. But he got to the floor of the gulch without injury to himself or the horse, and he stood for a few minutes, breathing heavily. He went then to the creek that trickled through here and fell beside it and drank deeply; and the horse drank, too, until he pulled the mount away.

He looked up at the rim and wondered if the sound of rolling rock had reached enemy ears. He waited, listening, and silence ruled this perfect Indian summer afternoon, and he might have been the first man on some far planet. Now he could ride again, and he mounted and headed on up the gulch, which here was not much more than a rocky slot. Excitement began growing in him, for another mile would bring him to the cave.

He told himself he must not let excitement rule him; he must be braced for disappointment. He had no real proof that Duke would be hiding there; he was going on guesswork. Not until yesterday had he really thought of the cave, yet the cave had come to mind in the boxcar, too, twined with all the memories of Duke; and thus it was as though the cave had drawn him across the last five years, and now the time left could be measured in minutes.

And so he rode through the holding silence, a silence suddenly broken by the raucous cawing of crows that rose in a black cluster from a tree and went their flapping way into the sky. Later he saw a badger go scurrying, and still later a porcupine waddled across the trail slowly, disdainfully, quilled lord of creation.

He knew every landmark now, every rock, every tree, remembered from childhood. He knew that shale slope ahead, marking the east end of the gulch; and when he climbed it, he would see the black maw of the cave. He found himself breathing hard. His horse whinnied then, and another horse, unseen, answered; and his heart seemed to stop beating; for if a horse was here, likely a man was here, and the man would be warned.

Peering, he saw the horse, picketed in the timber crowding the south wall of the gulch. It was unsaddled and no horse he remembered—a blaze-faced black— but when he rode closer, he saw that it wore the Boxed J brand. It grazed on a rope long enough to permit it to water at the creek; and by all that was sensible, it had to be Duke's horse.

Dismounting, he led his own horse deep into the thicket and tied it up and stood waiting, listening. No sound from the cave—no boots disturbing the shale slope before the cave. He ventured forward; he reached the foot of the slope and began carefully climbing. He took an eternity at this, certain now that Duke was above, certain that Duke had been alerted. He got to the top of the slope, and the high wide entrance to the cave was before him. His most defenseless moment would be when he walked through that opening with the light behind him and his silhouette sharply apparent to anyone within. He could have called out to Duke, naming himself and thus asking for Duke's mercy, but he wanted to be under no obligation to Duke. He stepped into the cave.

It was as if he had plunged into the pit of night. At first he was absolutely blinded, and as he took another step forward, he stumbled over the uneven, rocky floor. A pebble went rolling. He paused then and said, "Duke—?" low-voiced. No answer came. Duke must have gone somewhere afoot.

He waited for his eyes to grow accustomed to the gloom, and soon he made out the long narrow room that was the cave. He saw where a fire had been built not far from the entrance, and close by were Duke's saddle and blanket and a gunny-sack. When he bent for a closer look, he saw a tablet and a pencil near the saddle. Folded on top of the tablet was a note. He unfolded the note and carried it to the opening where he had light to read and instantly recognized Duke's handwriting.

The note bore no salutation and no signature, but it was plainly intended for Dorcas. He read it unabashed.

Midnight by my watch, and something must have happened or you'd have got here by now. I've been going crazy, holed up here and worrying. I started down the gulch as soon as it got dark, but I found Hatchet camped and blocking the way. Probably that's what's keeping you from reaching me.

I've staked out my horse because I think I can get past them on foot. If I can make it, I'll drift down the road a piece and hope to meet you coming. If we miss each other, and you somehow manage to reach here, please wait. I'll be back as soon as it is safe to make it.

He folded the note and dropped it. Duke, slipping out last night on foot, must have got safely past Hatchet's camp, for Hatchet had still been hunting him this morning. But how far down the road had Duke got? Far enough to have run into Sam Tull? He shook his head. He could picture Tull and Duke shooting it out at a moonlight meeting, but he still could not believe that Duke had put a bullet in Tull's back.

No matter. The important point was that Duke was gone from here but planned to return. The picketed horse was the proof that he hadn't yet made it back. Nothing to do now but wait for Duke, and he looked into the gunny-sack and found food—dry roast meat and drier bread, bacon, canned goods. He ate some of the bread and meat. He got out his jackknife and opened a can of tomatoes and drank the juice and fished out the pulp with his knife point and ate it. He felt tremendously renewed. He lay upon Duke's blanket then and pillowed his head on Duke's saddle, and presently he dozed . . .

He dreamed of Pru. He was in prison again, and Pru came to see him and tried to explain about Dorcas's not writing, but he didn't really listen to her, not caring what she said but only being glad that she had come. He awoke with a start to discover that it was much lighter in the cave. It was now late afternoon, with the sun tipped far west, and the rays slanting in here made a golden chamber of the place.

He stood up, angry with himself for his carelessness in having slept. But nothing had changed; he was still alone. He walked out of the cave and went far enough down the slope so he could see that Duke's horse still grazed. He climbed back into the cave. He thought of all the riders moving across the face of the mountain today—Hatchet on its relentless hunt; Gulley Jordan trying to reach here likely, and blocked, it would seem, since the old man hadn't made it. Maybe Gulley had run into Hatchet hands, too, and was taking some devious way. He thought of Duke, who might be anywhere, and of Dorcas, who hoped to marry him. He thought of Pru and hoped she was safe at home in Signal.

Restless, he began prowling the cave. On the walls were scratchings he and Duke had made in imitation of cave drawings they had seen in books. One was of their own conception, a six-legged horse. He went deep into the cave, far back toward its end, and found where a fire had burned long ago and guessed it had been one he and Duke had kindled. He looked down at the charred stubs of wood that had been patiently toted from the gulch, and he bent closer, drawn by something there in the debris that was no part of boyhood memory.

He lifted the object and held it, a partially-consumed carpetbag. He looked at it, knew it for what it was, and his pulse raced and his mouth went dry. He fumbled at the clasp. Inside he found a great wad of newspapers, scorched and half burned. He tore this wad apart and held one of the newspapers close to his eyes and made out the masthead. The Jupiter City *Journal*. He couldn't read the dateline in this light, but he didn't need to. He knew the date, for the meaning of his discovery was suddenly as clear to him as a landscape made sharp by a lightning flash on a stormy night.

The cave—always the cave! The cave, so exclusively his and Duke's in boyhood—the cave, recalled by both of them when Duke had turned fugitive night before last and he had taken Duke's trail yesterday. And the cave had been remembered another time, too. Five years ago, when he had camped higher up, returning from Jupiter City with this very carpetbag and had been attacked by a masked rider who had fled with the carpetbag—fled here and lighted a fire and left the carpetbag to burn, though it hadn't burned completely.

And now, with the thing in his hands, he was thinking of last night at Brewsters' and what Gulley had told him in the hope of wringing mercy from him, of how Duke had gambled and lost heavily at Jupiter City and how the suspicion had been born in Gulley that Duke had sent Ry Buckner home with a carpetbag of worthless contents and then had robbed him on the trail so that the truth would not be revealed by delivery of the carpetbag to Gulley. Here was the clinching piece of evidence, this carpetbag in this cave.

He let the scorched object drop, and in him then was the thought born in the courtroom the night before last, that there was a thing sadder than the death of a friend, and that was the death of a friendship. He had pondered two questions: had Duke framed him, and if so, why? He had the answer to the first. As for the second, there was Dorcas wooed and won, with a rival removed when the gates of Deer Lodge had clanged shut.

He felt the beat of anger in his temples. He had freed himself from anger when he had looked down upon a conquered Sam Tull and realized why he had gone at Tull with fist and fury, but that had been before this last bit of damning evidence had come to hand, this last piece of a puzzle had fallen into place.

He remembered Duke in Jupiter City and his pleading with Duke to hit the home trail, as he had followed Duke from one saloon and gambling hall to another. He remembered the nights Duke had given him the slip and how finally Duke had handed him the carpetbag and told him to take it along home, promising he'd hit the trail himself shortly. And at that very time Duke had known what the carpetbag held, and known, too, what he must do to keep it from being delivered.

Anger grew in him, and he did not try to fight it. He let the fierce joy of anger claim him.

He turned then, wrenched from chaotic thinking by a warning sound. He turned, hearing shale rattle as someone came up the slope to the cave's mouth. Gulley?

Dorcas? Some prowling hand from Hatchet? But no, that was Duke silhouetted there in the opening—no mistaking his build—and he faced toward Duke and drew his gun at the same time and stood waiting.

13 : Came McQueen

He let Duke come through the opening, for he knew that Duke, blinded by sunlight, couldn't see him. He brought the gun up level, covering Duke; and then he saw the second silhouette, the one behind Duke's; and he drew in a sharp breath, for Dorcas was here, coming into the cave on Duke's heels.

He hadn't counted on Dorcas, yet her presence was not surprising when he remembered the note Duke had left. Duke, sneaking past Hatchet's camp afoot in the hours beyond midnight, must have drifted on down the road as he'd planned, drifted into the dawn and a meeting with Dorcas, riding up from the Brewster place. Probably they'd both been near him before he'd quit the road and taken to the back country. And now they were here.

Her coming need make no difference, he told himself. He said in a level voice, "Stop where you are, Duke. You, too, Dorcas. Don't try for your gun, Duke!"

Duke jerked in astonishment. "All right, Ry," he said. "Dorcas told me you were on my trail."

"Unlatch your gun-belt, Duke. That's right—slow and easy. Let it drop. Now hook your toe under it and kick it this way. Fine."

Dorcas looked at the discarded gun-belt on the rocky floor. "So you made it, Ry," she said. "With Hatchet hands all over the slope, you made it. I should have known."

"Seems you made it, too," he said.

"Get on with it," Duke said sullenly. "You've hunted me and you've found me. Where do you go from here, Ry?"

He moved toward Duke, wanting a real look at him. There was light enough. He had expected to find Duke's weak, handsome face five years older. What he hadn't expected was to find lines of suffering there. Duke looked like a man who had been through some long sickness, and the disarming thing was that even though anger still beat in him, he felt a stab of pity for Duke. He put his mind against this. He thought of that burned carpetbag, wanting to summon full anger again; and he asked stonily, "Do you remember the courtroom, Duke?"

"Yes, and the words you said to me as they led you out. About the man with the mask being my build. You'd guessed then, hadn't you, Ry?"

"Not for certain. The thing I kept remembering was that you didn't protest. Then one by one the pieces began to fall into place. Your wanting to hang around Jupiter City once we'd been paid for those cattle and the crew had gone home. The gambling you must have done on nights when you gave me the slip. Your giving me the carpetbag, finally, but saying you wanted to stay a couple days more. What you really did was follow me and get the carpetbag and bring it here and try to burn it. But I didn't find out that last fact till just now."

"But meantime you'd guessed and were hating me, I reckon."

"I used to lie awake in the prison nights and think about you, Duke. I'd picture us meeting again someday, and I'd even worked out the words I'd say words cal culated to draw the truth out of you and then make you mad enough to fight. That fight was going to be with guns, and I'd picked out the button on your shirt to aim at. It made good dreaming till it went sour. And then I knew I couldn't do it, given the chance."

The sullen tone went out of Duke's voice, and in its place came the first hope, the first eagerness. "Why, Riley? What changed your mind?"

"Everything that had been between us," Buckner said. "All the good memories weighed against the one bad one. I was the gambler's kid whose father had died under suspicion of having cheated. I was the boy who'd needed a friend more than I needed the hope of heaven. You came along and were that friend. No, it wasn't the things you did like seeing that I ate when I was hungry and got a job on Boxed J when I was old enough. I'd have made out, regardless. It was just that when I needed you in my life, you were there. Does that make sense?"

Softly: "I reckon, Ry."

"That's when I began seeing that I owed you plenty and that maybe five years out of life was one way of paying back. I began hoping I'd added up the thing wrong and maybe you weren't the masked man who hit my camp. Or if you were, you had some good reason for what you did. Then the only thing that mattered was not whether you'd double-crossed me, but *why?* Why would you have done such a thing to me, of all people? That's what put me on your trail, Duke. Everybody jumped to the notion that I was out howling for vengeance, while all I wanted was to ask that question. But maybe I got the answer yesterday. Maybe you put me in prison to get Dorcas."

"On my word, Ry, it wasn't that!"

"Then why, man?"

Duke shook his head. "A fellow takes a wrong step, figuring he'll take that one and no more. Then he finds that the first step has forced him to a second and a third. You wouldn't know about that, Ry, because you were always strong where I was weak. I can't tell you the why of what I did, not so it will make sense to you."

"I think you'd better try, Duke."

"I did considerable helling around in the old days, you'll remember. I even got mixed up in a few things you didn't know about, because I was too ashamed to tell you about them. There was a time, for instance, when I ran up a two thousand dollar gambling debt that Gulley had to pay. I'd got to the end of my rope when we were sent to Jupiter with those cattle. Gulley laid it out plain the night before we left. One more slip on my part would be the last—he'd disown me, cut me off at the pockets. Maybe he was bluffing. Looking back now, I think he was, because I've always been his soft spot. Anyway, he had me scared—plenty scared—but still I did a foolish thing."

"Yes," Buckner said. "You started gambling at Jupiter."

"With my own money, Ry. You were with me that first night, and you'll remember that I won. That's what gave me the notion I was going to come home with two thousand dollars in winnings and pay Gulley back. But the next night I lost, so I began digging into the cattle money. After that I won a little, lost a lot, won a little more. Oh, those Jupiter City sharks knew how to string along a sucker! All the while you kept prodding me to get along home. Finally I gave you a carpetbag full of newspapers. The last of the money was in my pocket. I was going to clean up that night and overtake you on the trail and tell you the truth, and we'd have a good laugh about it and then ride home together with the money. By midnight I was cleaned except for a couple of hundred dollars."

"Later Gulley guessed that you'd gambled the money away," Buckner said. "He told me so last night."

"I walked the streets of Jupiter afterwards, Ry. I was crazy, desperate. I thought of trying a bank holdup, but I couldn't bring myself to that. I thought of catching up with you, telling you the truth. Maybe the two of us could figure a way out. I began to wonder if you'd looked into the carpetbag and already knew. Then it hit me that you likely hadn't, and that if I masked myself and got that bag away from you, I'd be in the clear. Some unknown would be blamed for the robbery."

Buckner nodded. "Rider X, McQueen called him."

"I hit your camp with you rolled into blankets and fogged with sleep. I thought of the cave and fetched the bag here. I left it burning and lit out for Boxed J."

"Yes," Buckner said, his voice hardening, "and there you planted that last couple of hundred in my bunk. With serial numbers on those bills to identify them as being cattle sale money!"

"Yes, Ry. I did that, too."

"But why?" Buckner asked explosively. "All the rest of it I can understand now. The first wrong step of risking your own money gambling. The second step of using Boxed J money. The idea of making the loss look like robbery. But once you got that bag away from me, you were in the clear, and I was in the clear. Rider X would have got the blame. But then you nailed down the lid on me by planting money in my bunk. Why, man?"

"I don't know," Duke said miserably. "I got back to the ranch just before dawn. I found a bottle I'd cached out in the barn and sat there in the dark sucking on it, thinking crazy thoughts. Mostly about what Gulley had threatened. I remember being afraid that Gulley would see through the whole thing, figure it was something we had rigged together. Thoughts kept going round and round in my head. Then I sneaked into the bunkhouse and planted that last two hundred under your tick. I can't tell you why."

"Maybe I can," Dorcas said.

Buckner hadn't looked at her till now. He had kept his eyes on Duke's face, watching his agony, his desperation. He had warmed some, listening to Duke and coming at last to full understanding of what had moved Duke five years ago, finding some faith in Duke again because Duke was being honest. Everything squared except that last thing.

"In bookkeeping," Dorcas said, "an account is debits

and credits and a balance until a last entry is made that closes the account. Then we rule it up. We draw a line under it, and that finishes the matter. Duke wanted the account of the missing money ruled closed. Not until that happened would he be truly free of worry. By planting that money in your bunk, you'd be blamed and the account closed. And having done that, he was stuck with it."

Duke nodded slowly. "I never thought of it that way. Then or since. But it's so, I guess, the way Dorcas puts it. I went through hell in the days before you were sentenced. I went through hell the first years you were in prison. Once I went to the courthouse and walked halfway up the stairs to the county attorney's office. I was going to spill the whole thing to Granville Cross. My nerve ran out before I got to his door."

"And I stayed in prison because of that! Can't you understand, Duke? It's not the five years I begrudge. The thing that rankles is knowing you might have faced up to the music and didn't."

"All right," Duke said. "I didn't have the guts when it would have mattered. No changing that. Do I buckle on my gun-belt and we stand even and take it from there?"

"What am I supposed to do, Duke? Pin a rose on you and walk out of here?"

Dorcas said, "Would it make any difference to you, Ry, to know that I'm his wife now? We were married this afternoon."

He heard her and shook his head as a man does who has been struck hard. He had been too concerned with here and now, with the truth to be learned, to give thought to what might have happened since Duke and

Dorcas had met. Vaguely he had supposed that they had been dodging Hatchet through the day and so had been delayed getting back here to pick up Duke's horse. He stared at Dorcas.

"We met very near the spot where I found you last night, Ry," she said. "We were going to come up here and get Duke's horse; but when we ran into a couple of Hatchet hands, we took to the brush to get away. After that, we kept working west along game trails."

He nodded. "And you went to wherever Pru's note said the Reverend Jones would be."

"That's right. The Swain place, where Reverend Jones held a prayer meeting last night. He was still there this morning, and his boy; and Pru was there, too. She rode out from town early. The old couple at the ranch hadn't heard yet about Duke's being wanted, and they witnessed the marriage, too. We started back here to get Duke's horse right after that."

"Duke," Buckner asked, "did you meet up with Sam Tull last night?"

"No," Duke said, "I didn't. Why?"

"Never mind that now. The two of you came through Timmerman on your way here?"

"Nobody there, Ry," Dorcas said. "I remembered your warning. We nearly ran into Hatchet riders three times on the way, but their camp was deserted."

"It won't be come night."

"There's time left," Dorcas said. "We can all get through the gulch before then if we leave soon. I want Duke to surrender to the law. I've talked to him about it all the way up here. McQueen thinks he can get off on the grounds of defending his property. I want you to forget whatever fight you've got against Duke, Ry. Whether I've the right to ask that or not, I'm asking it. Because he's my husband now, and I want him alive."

He didn't know what to say. He had learned too much too quickly for all of it to be straight in his head; and though he now understood what had driven Duke five years ago, there was still the one stickler, the fact that Duke, ruling the matter closed, had left it closed. That was what kept him from forgiving Duke, yet he wanted desperately to do so, and in his mind ran an echo of something Virgil McQueen had said night before last. "You want to believe in Duke because he was that close to you that believing in him is believing in yourself." And he remembered the words the Reverend Jones had smeared on the canvas of his wagon: JUDGE NOT, THAT YE BE NOT JUDGED.

"Ry," Duke said urgently, "you've got no cause for a grudge against Dorcas. Let her leave, Ry. Right now."

"Before Hatchet comes back to the gulch? Is that what's worrying you?"

"I don't care about myself," Duke said.

Buckner sighed, his choice made. "You can both go," he said. "I didn't come here for blood. I came for a truth. I've got it. I suppose I should be giving you both my blessing. Don't expect that of me. I'm remembering that you didn't quite get to Cross's office, Duke."

"Not that other time, Ry. But by tomorrow morning at the latest, he'll have the whole story."

"No, Duke. You're full of shame and self-reproach now that you're facing me. But you'll think twice once I'm out of your sight. And Dorcas will help you change your mind because she'll want you in less trouble, not more."

"Too late for that," Duke said. "I put it in writing, and it's on its way to the county attorney's office right now."

This surprised Dorcas as much as it did Buckner. He could see that by the way her mouth fell open. Duke turned to her. "Honey," he said, "I left Boxed J panicked the night before last, nothing in my mind but Lark Rigby gone down with his face bloody and me with my gun in my hand. I'd been in trouble before, but not like that. I was on the run, and it would be a hangrope if I got caught. And that's when I saw that the least I could do was square away that old business involving Ry."

Her eyes widened. "So you stopped at Pothook and borrowed writing materials! McQueen told me that."

"True," he said. "And yesterday I sat up here and wrote a long letter to Granville Cross. I admitted shooting Lark Rigby, which Sam Tull was going to tell him anyway. And I told the whole truth about that business five years ago. It won't rub out the time Ry spent in prison, but it will square me with myself."

"But you said the letter was on its way. How?"

"I gave it to Pru at the Swain place, Dorcas. I asked her to deliver it to no one but Cross himself."

"Duke," she said, "that was a foolish thing to do!"

"No," Duke said. "It will give me my first real night's sleep in over five years."

"But when you stand trial for shooting Lark, Cross will bring up the matter of your confession, and you'll have two charges to face. McQueen showed me the way out of one. Do you think a jury will forgive you for the other just because you happened to get remorseful five years later? Duke, you're such an idiot!"

"Can't you see that I had to do it?" he pleaded. "And that I couldn't tell you till now because I couldn't hope that you'd understand?"

She stayed silent and thoughtful for a long moment. "I guess I do understand," she said then.

"You'd better get started back," Duke urged. "Not much time left."

"Come with me, Duke," she said. "Turn yourself in."

"No," he said. "We've been over that. And if there'll be two charges against me, that's twice as much reason for staying hid."

"You're making another mistake, Duke."

"You get riding while there's time, Dorcas," Duke insisted. "Let me talk to Ry about it and sleep on the matter. Will you do that?"

Buckner expected her to argue further, but instead she shrugged. It struck Buckner that she was now impatient to be gone from here but was concealing her impatience.

"I'll meet you here when it's safe, Duke," she said. "Come with me now and get those blankets I fetched."

She turned toward the opening, and Duke followed her. Buckner watched them go and suddenly realized he still held his gun. He dropped it into his holster. He felt drained and weak, but happy. He thought of that letter on its way to Granville Cross and knew the source of his happiness. He waited for Duke to come back. Presently Duke loomed in the cave opening.

He came in and dropped the blanket roll. He did not

look at Buckner; he did not offer his hand. There was this awkwardness between them, and it would remain for a while, Buckner guessed. Duke started digging into the gunny-sack. "You rustle some firewood; I'll cook us some grub," he said.

"Sure, Duke," Buckner said. "Sure."

He went out and worked his way down the shale slope and into the timber and found a deadfall and broke branches from it. He came back with an armload and saw that Duke had picked up his gun-belt and buckled it on. Duke got a fire going and took a skillet from the gunny-sack and began frying bacon. He did this in silence and they ate in silence, and not until they had finished did Duke really look at him. "What do *you* think, Ry?" Duke asked then. "Should I turn myself in?"

Buckner didn't answer. He stood up suddenly, and his hand fell toward his gun, for he had heard the rattle of shale, ever so faint. Only one man in the county could move as silently as that, and he dropped his hand from the gun, knowing it was too late—too late for the try, too late for Duke.

"Easy, Duke," he said. "He's got us covered."

He judged from Duke's face that Duke had guessed, without turning, that it was Virgil McQueen there in the opening looking at them in the wash of the firelight.

14 : The Struggle

Mighty hard it was, Dorcas had discovered, to ride slowly through the gulch when her compelling need was to gallop. She must remember, though, that trouble could lie ahead where Hatchet camped, and so she had to be wary of each turn of the trail. But still the cry clamored in her to hurry, hurry!

Not long ago she had kissed Duke good-by in the timber below the cave, kissed him hastily, wondering if he suspected the real reason she was so eager to be on her way. Ry had sensed her impatience, she felt certain; there had been something about the way Ry had looked at her. But probably not Duke, her husband. Odd how hard it was to get used to the idea that she was now Mrs. Duke Jordan. Here it was her wedding night, but she and Duke would spend it far apart. That had to be because she must get Duke's confession, if possible, and destroy it before it could reach Granville Cross's hand. She must!

A lost cause? Pru should be long since into Signal, her errand completed. Pru, who had faithfully been on hand for the wedding but had stood wooden-faced through the ceremony, showing neither approval nor disapproval. Just when had Duke managed to give his letter to her? While that old couple had been buzzing about, insisting that everyone stay for a sort of wedding feast, she guessed. Pru had started for town right after that. No chance, likely, of beating Pru to the county attorney, but she could hope. Cross might just be out of Signal today; his business took him to the four corners of the county. If only she dared hurry now!

Thank heavens that Duke, fearing Hatchet, had insisted that she go at once. Duke wouldn't like her real reason for hurrying away. She could see now what being Mrs. Duke Jordan would entail in all the years ahead. She would have to be the steel and strength for both of them, and the wisdom. A sentimental fool, Duke, an inherently decent person who would forever tangle his twine and then tangle it twice over trying to extricate himself. A man who would always take the wrong way to do a right thing.

She sighed. For his very weaknesses she loved Duke, and she could understand why Ry, at the end, had forgiven him. She thought of the two of them back there in the cave, peace between them; that was the only good come out of Duke's bungling. All Ry had needed was the knowledge of that silly confession letter. Let the confession be destroyed by any hand but Duke's and nothing would be changed between Ry and Duke.

She *had* to get hold of that letter.

The sun had gone; and though the valley below would lie golden in the afterglow, twilight crowded the mountain slope, and darkness would soon gather in the gulch. Now she rounded a turn to see a man sitting his saddle in the trail ahead. She had been wary, but not wary enough. A scream built in her throat; then she recognized the man. No Hatchet hand he, but Sheriff Virgil McQueen, a lesser evil.

"All right, Dorcas," he said quietly, "we'll waste no time sparring. You left him up there at the cave, him and Ry Buckner?"

She reined up. "You know about the cave?"

"I remembered it finally. I got to it before noon today. Duke's horse was there, but he wasn't. I read a note he'd left for you. I've patrolled between Hatchet's camp and the cave since, waiting and watching. Buckner showed up this afternoon, and then you and Duke went by here riding double not long ago. I'm going to bring him in now, girl."

Astonished, she said, "But you could have thrown a gun on him when we were on our way up!"

"It wasn't quite four o'clock, Dorcas. We made a bargain, remember? I've kept my end of it."

"Believe me, I argued with him!" she insisted. "Given time, I can bring him around. Can you give me twenty-four hours more?"

"I reckon not," he said. "I just wanted you to know I played fair."

"Are you arresting me, too?"

He shook his head. "Nor Ry Buckner, unless he interferes. Just be sure you don't try to turn back to warn Duke."

She'd been thinking fast all this while. She begrudged the moments he was holding her here, knowing that Hatchet might bottle up the gulch meanwhile, knowing that time could count in her getting to Granville Cross ahead of Pru, if that were still possible. Half a cause lost once Duke was arrested, but perhaps half a cause still to be won. She said, "I'm heading for town. Tell me this: do you still believe he has a chance in court?"

He shrugged. "It's as possible as it was yesterday. Better he'd surrendered, though."

She said, "Too late for that. I thank you for the twenty-four hours. I'll give you no trouble."

He pulled his horse aside to let her pass. "Good girl," he said.

She rode around him and headed on. She felt him watching after her, but when she did venture to look back, he was gone from sight. Should she turn and follow him to the cave? For a moment the temptation was strong, her heart crying out to Duke, but she knew where her own course lay. The shadows were deepening, and Hatchet would be coming to the gathering place soon.

She rode on. She reached Hatchet's campsite and turned weak with relief, finding it as deserted as when she and Duke had passed here earlier, heading in the opposite direction. Some picketed horses, Hatchet remounts, grazed the meadow. A pile of gear stood yonder, and a small tent, probably for Spence Rigby. She skirted the camp and got into timber again and found herself tense, certain that at any moment she would hear the crash of horses along the trail ahead. She reached the rocky slot.

Soon she was out onto the ancient road and raising her horse to a gallop. Deep dark was coming on, and a half mile below the turnoff she charged past two shadowy horsemen headed uphill. One seemed to pull his mount about, to give chase; the second shouted something at the first, and she guessed she had been recognized. She quirted her horse and rode recklessly. After a while she felt certain she wasn't pursued.

The horse was lathered when she reached the Brewsters' place, and night had got to the valley ahead of her. She walked the horse for a time, impatient at the pace. She reached Pothook an hour later and changed horses there, not offering any explanation. Now she could gallop again, and she pushed the horse by starlight, pushed it relentlessly, and got another fresh mount at Anchor 4. She could see the crew gathered in the lamplighted mess hall, and only then did she realize she was hungry. She headed out from Anchor 4 in a straight line for Signal, riding hard, no thought in her but to finish and finish soon.

Nine o'clock, she judged, when she hit town and pulled the horse to a trot along Bottom Street. The lighted Frontier showed horses at its hitchrail; and when she passed the mercantile, she saw her mother moving about by lamplight. She peered, looking for Pru. She rode on to the courthouse corner. No light tonight in McQueen's quarters, but two upper windows glowed, one in the treasurer's office, the other in the county attorney's. She got off the horse and took a step and almost fell.

She was praying; the words were a jumble in her mind, but at the core of them lay her plea: *Let me have got here in time! Please, God!*

She climbed the huge front steps and tried the ponderous door and found it locked. She pounded on the door, shouting, "Open up! Open up!" She pounded again and again. She turned away then, determined to get some small pebbles and throw them at the nearest of those lighted windows. Someone, working late, would surely come and open up. She took a step and heard the door groan behind her. She faced about and saw Pike Fisher, Cross's ancient clerk, peering out.

"Granville? Where is he?" she demanded.

"Out of town," Fisher said.

"Where did he go? When did he leave?"

"About noon. He had two, three errands in the valley. First was at Hatchet. Tull's bunch buried Lark Rigby yesterday morning without waiting for a coroner's inquest. Seeing as there was no argument about how Lark got killed, Hatchet probably figured an inquest wasn't needed. Especially since they were itching to hit Duke's trail. Granville figures we'd better get an affidavit from Tull, stating the facts."

She was afraid she was going to faint. She put a hand against the unopened half of the door to steady herself. "Thank you!" she cried. "Oh, thank you!"

He regarded her curiously. "What's got the Lane family in such a sweat to see Granville? Your sister was here late this afternoon looking for him, too. I told Pru he'd likely be back tomorrow."

She didn't answer him. She groped down the steps and mounted the horse and walked it up the side street that led to Maw's house. She swung down before the frame building and dropped the reins over the gate post. A lamp burned low in the parlor, but she found no one there when she entered. She called, "Pru—?" and from her bedroom Pru's voice called back in surprise, "Dorcas? What are you doing here? I'm coming."

Pru had heard the front door open, then slam shut. Her first thought was that Maw had come home from whatever puttering around the store she'd been doing this evening. Then Dorcas called. Dorcas here, on her wedding night? She had left Dorcas at that west-end ranch-house with Duke.

The odd thing was that she'd just been thinking about Dorcas, or rather, about the wedding. She had ridden in from the valley this afternoon and gone directly to the county attorney's office, impelled by the urgency in Duke's voice when he had given her that letter out at the Swain place. When she had found Cross absent from his office, she had gone to the store and helped Maw, fending off Maw's questions and surmises the while. They had had supper here at home, and she had parried more questions and been glad when Maw had decided to go back to the store and replenish some shelves. Only then had she found time to think about today.

She had sat at her dresser primping, not really having her mind on this but just sort of dreaming before the glass, remembering the parlor of the little ranch-house and Duke and Dorcas standing before Reverend Jones, Duke solemn and scared but somehow looking more of a man than before, as though he had settled something with himself and could square his shoulders because of that. Afterwards, when he'd given her the letter and the hasty, whispered instructions for its delivery, she'd wondered if the letter had anything to do with the change in him.

Dorcas had been solemn, too, during the ceremony, but not scared. The Reverend Jones had had a sort of troubled look as though not rightly sure he should be tying the knot. The reverend, she had surmised, knew about the murder charge against Duke, so likely questioned whether the wedding was fitting and proper. Something of a poser for a man whose wagon bore the legend JUDGE NOT, THAT YE BE NOT JUDGED. His son had served as the second witness, though not really needed with the old couple present. She'd smiled, remembering Swain looking awkward in a necktie put on for the occasion, his wife sniffling loudly, though she didn't really know either Dorcas or Duke but evidently cried at weddings from habit.

There had been an awkward moment when the time came to pay the preacher and it developed that Duke had fled Boxed J so fast he hadn't taken any money along, which showed how rattled he'd been. Dorcas, who had provided the ring, pressed some silver dollars on Reverend Jones. *Buying herself a husband,* Pru had thought, *having shopped for the best bargain.* But that had been unjust. Dorcas really loved Duke, as had been plain to see when she turned her face to be kissed at the end of the ceremony and had looked protective and motherly and somehow luminous, not at all like the Dorcas she'd always known.

But now, amazingly, Dorcas was here; and when Pru came into the parlor she saw her sister standing there, looking hard-used and almost ready to fall, yet at the same time looking fierce enough to fight a mountain lion, her eyes wild with whatever need had brought her.

"That letter," Dorcas said sharply. "The one Duke

gave you to hand to Granville Cross. You've still got it?"

"Why, yes," Pru said. "Granville wasn't in town."

"Give it to me," Dorcas demanded.

Pru stiffened. "Duke said I was to hand it to Granville. And to nobody else."

"Haven't you guessed what's in it?"

"Something about that trouble with Lark Rigby the other night, I suppose. Duke's side of the story."

"More than that, Pru. It has a full confession about what happened five years ago, telling how Duke robbed Ry Buckner on the trail home and then framed him."

Pru drew in a deep breath. Suddenly she was so happy she wanted to sing, yet whatever bond she was freed from was one she hadn't known existed. Ry cleared! Ry proved innocent at last, and yet she had never condemned Ry in her mind or thought different of him because he had gone to prison; still this was a great thing, knowing that he needn't have gone.

"I should have guessed all along," she said. "We all should have. Some people thought Ry innocent and suspected Duke. Now everybody will know the truth!"

"No," Dorcas said. "I've got to you in time. That letter must be destroyed."

Pru was startled. "That would be for Duke to say. He chose to write it."

"Pru," Dorcas said, "you're being as big a fool as Duke. That business of five years ago is dead now; Ry is out of prison and it's all over and done with. Will you tell me what earthly good it will do for Duke to put a second strike against himself when already he has a murder charge to face?"

"It will make an old wrong right," Pru said. "It will make Ry really free."

"All Ry wanted, all he returned for, was to bridge back to Duke, if he could. I left the two of them a few hours ago. They are friends again. Ask Ry when you see him if that isn't enough."

"I see," Pru said, and she was growing angry. "You want a husband free of trouble, so you want Duke to have every chance in court. You want that at any cost. Ry doesn't matter, and Duke doesn't matter really; only your selfishness matters. The town was right—Martha Castner and all the others who threw things up to Maw. They guessed what you were after when you bought a marriage license with Duke on the run. They said you wanted to marry Duke before he got hanged, so that Boxed J would be yours when Gulley dies. I know you, Dorcas. I know that nothing has ever mattered to you but getting hold of the almighty dollar. But this time what somebody else wants is going to count. I mean that letter and what Duke wanted done with it!"

Dorcas stepped back as though she had been struck, anger coloring her face and her eyes blazing. Then she shook her head slowly. "Maybe I deserved that, Pru," she said. "That doesn't make it hurt less, coming from you. Maybe you were too young to remember Paw dead and Maw starting the first store in a shack and the days when we went hungry and the nights when we slept cold. That was when I first realized that what you really want you should go after. And that was when I promised myself the Lanes would see better days. Not only me. You. Maw. Starting today, I'm mistress of Boxed J. Not the hired bookkeeper—the lady of the house. If I was in no hurry to marry Duke until I saw I might lose the chance, the fact remains that my marrying him means the beginning of a good day. Not only for me. For you and Maw, too. That's what I always wanted— the best for the Lane family."

"Except," Pru said, "that you never bothered to ask us whether that was what *we* wanted or whether we'd quibble at any part of the price. I'm quibbling now, Dorcas, when it means that Duke's letter has to be destroyed."

Dorcas took a step toward her, anger on her cheeks again. "Where is that letter?" she demanded.

"I won't tell you!" Pru flared, but in spite of herself she glanced toward the bedroom.

Dorcas saw that glance and started for her bedroom. Pru moved quickly, blocking the doorway. Dorcas looked beyond her, eyes widening, for the letter stood on the dresser, propped against the mirror. Dorcas reached for her. She felt her sister's fingers close on her shoulder and Dorcas try to hurl her aside. She got her arms around Dorcas, and the two of them began swaying and struggling, fierce as two cats. She flung her weight against Dorcas, and they went down to roll on the floor.

There was no scratching or biting, and yet they were pitted against each other relentlessly. There was no shrieking; they struggled silently, Pru finding more strength in Dorcas than she had expected; but Dorcas's real advantage was something of the mind. Pru, the younger, had never before truly defied Dorcas, and it seemed strange now and terrible to be exerting all her strength to best Dorcas. But slowly she was pinning Dorcas to the floor, and then Dorcas ceased struggling.

"All right, Pru," Dorcas said in an even voice. "You win."

Pru got up and darted to the dresser and took the letter. She turned to see Dorcas sitting upright on the floor. She melted at that sight and said, close to crying, "I'm sorry, Dorcas. Believe me, I'm sorry."

"I'm sorry, too," Dorcas said. She raised a hand and brushed her cheek, and something about that gesture flung Pru in memory to a time long forgotten. She saw herself a tot at a party one of the Galloway sisters had given, and Dorcas coming in late, blonde and pretty in her best frock but with a smear of coal dust on her cheek, and the Galloway girl shrieking with laughter and pointing to the smear, drawing everyone's attention, and Dorcas suddenly red-faced and hurt, brushing at her cheek just as she had done now. And remembering, Pru understood everything and forgave Dorcas everything.

"Just the same, I'm taking this letter to Granville, Dorcas," she said.

"I won't beg," Dorcas said. "What it really amounts to, I guess, is each of us fighting for the man she loves. You see, I knew how you felt about Ry in the old days, when he used to come here courting me. It showed on you, Pru, even then. And tonight you've proved it."

Pru stared and nearly made denial. Just last night she had been certain that she wasn't in love with Ry Buckner, but now, with Dorcas insisting she was, she suddenly knew that it was true and had indeed been true for a long time. That was why she had been glad last night that it was Duke whom Dorcas had intended marrying, not Ry. And that was why the delivery of Duke's confession was so important to her, for Ry's sake.

She fled across the room and seized a coat from the hall rack and flung it over her shoulders and left the house, the letter in her hand. She had the feeling that Dorcas, given time to recover her breath and her ambition, might again be after her. She saw the horse at the gate, a mount Dorcas must have borrowed at Anchor 4, for that brand was on it. She gathered up the reins and climbed to the saddle and urged the horse along the street, remembering that she'd been told that Granville Cross had headed out to Hatchet. She would hit that road and hope to find him. Tonight. She could not feel safe again until she had put Duke's letter into Cross's hand.

15 : Gulley Empties a Gun

In Buckner, seeing McQueen step into the cave, gun in hand, the fear rose that Duke would make a play and die doing it. He read the desperation in Duke's face; and he knew Duke so thoroughly, the moral cowardice of his friend and the physical courage, that he could anticipate Duke's reaction. Duke was the kind to act first and think afterwards. Likely that was what had happened at the Strip fence when Lark Rigby had gone down under Duke's gun. And that was what could happen now, with the difference that the advantage was McQueen's. Duke would never get his hand to his holster. Yet his eyes showed such an intent, and his hand twitched convulsively, and Buckner said again, sharply, "Easy, Duke!"

"That's right," McQueen said. "Don't make me kill you." He came another step into the cave, the firelight touching that implacable face. "End of the trail, Duke. Now stand up and shuck that gun-belt."

Still the wildness, the desperation, showed in Duke's face, and his choice wasn't quite made. Buckner saw

Duke's eyes begging him for some sign, some wisdom beyond Duke's own; and he nodded. "Better do as he says, Duke."

Standing up slowly and as slowly unbuckling the gunbelt, Duke let it drop, then kicked it aside. "Getting to be a habit," he said. "One question, Virg. Coming here, you must have met Dorcas. Is she all right?"

"I met her," McQueen said. "She wanted another twenty-four hours to talk you into surrendering. But that game's played out."

"I don't give a damn about that!" Duke exploded. "What I want to know is whether she got past Hatchet's camp."

"Likely. We'll soon know. We'll be running that gantlet ourselves."

Buckner shook his head. "Think twice, McQueen. Dorcas is in no real danger, compared with Duke. Hatchet may have grabbed her and be trying to get her to lead them to Duke, but they'll never budge her in a million years, and they wouldn't try rough stuff on a woman. Spence Rigby's too cautious for that. But if they get Duke, it will be different. You know about Rigby's hangtree fever. You put the name to it. Better we hole up here till tomorrow when Hatchet is scattered over the mountain again."

"No," McQueen said stonily, "we try it tonight. I do my resting only when I've shut a cell door on Duke." He stared thoughtfully at Buckner. "I told you, remember, that come the showdown, I might find you on Duke's side of the fence. Is that the way it stands?"

"We settled our differences, McQueen. But that isn't the question. Man, there's no way out of the gulch by night except straight through! I'd have sent Dorcas up the slope otherwise, but I came in by way of the back country, and it's tough enough by daylight. Better to chance Hatchet's camp. But we don't have to do that until it's safer tomorrow."

"*You* don't have to chance anything," McQueen said pointedly. "You can stay here, if you like. I've got no claim on you unless you interfere."

"If you take Duke through, I go with you," Buckner said. "I told you we settled our differences." He thought of that letter put in Pru's hand. "The slate's clean, and I do what I'd be doing five years ago. I back him."

He saw Duke's shoulders straighten; he saw Duke turn younger. "No need, Ry," Duke said. "Best you keep out of it."

"I'm already in it, Duke. I'm not so popular with Hatchet myself."

McQueen said stubbornly, "We head out of here. Now. While there's still hope we can get through."

"No," Buckner said. "We don't."

"Maybe he's right, Ry," Duke said. "Let's try for town and get it over with. He's got me; and now that he has, maybe I'm glad. And maybe there's a chance for me in court, like Dorcas said. Hatchet catching me alone would be one thing. But they'd think twice about trying to take a prisoner from the law."

"Duke," Buckner said intently, "a man's reputation is his armor only as long as there's no crack in it. McQueen's has got a crack a mile wide. How many people have seen it I don't know, but one man has. Spence Rigby, who is dead set on hanging you. Ask McQueen if it isn't so. And ask him how much backing down Hatchet will do."

McQueen said without rancor, "All right, Ry. You've sized it up and told it true, but we're still better off getting out of here, if we hurry. Because there's one thing you've overlooked. Hatchet's out to comb the hills. So far they haven't ridden this way. This seems to be a dead-end gulch, a place a fugitive would avoid, and they don't know about the cave. The opening can't be seen till a man climbs that shale slope. Right?"

"Right."

"Then let's suppose that Dorcas found a few Hatchet hands returned to camp when she hit there. Let's suppose they grabbed her and tried to get her to say where Duke's hiding. Granted she wouldn't talk, and granted they wouldn't dare treat her rough, still they'd be mindful that they'd found her coming *down* the gulch. Now wouldn't that get them to wondering why she was up here? Can't you see that they might be riding this way right now?"

"True, all of it," Buckner said. "But either they didn't see Dorcas and aren't concerned with this dead end, or they saw her and are already on their way. And if they're coming, we're better off forted up here."

"Something to that," Duke agreed.

McQueen leveled his gun, his voice hardening. "I call the tune," he said. "I'm gambling that Dorcas got clear and that we'll get clear. I'm done with arguing. Buckner, I warned you night before last that if you sided against the law, I'd bring you along with Duke. You can shuck your gun-belt, too. You're under arrest."

"And if I tell you to go to hell?"

"Don't do it. This time I didn't leave my gun on a table. It's lined on your brisket, and the smoke of it will cover any crack in my armor you think you're seeing. Now shuck that gun-belt!"

Buckner stared, and this was like the other night when he had looked at McQueen in the sheriff's quarters after Spence Rigby had left and, looking, had realized the depth of McQueen's desperation and seen how time had worn away the rock. McQueen was even more desperate now. Knowing this, Buckner shrugged, fumbled at his belt and let it drop. He toed it in McQueen's direction.

McQueen, moving carefully, his tall, angular shadow flung dancing upon the cave wall by the dying firelight, picked up the two gun-belts and looped them over his left arm. He gestured with his gun. "Let's go," he said.

Ry and Duke came out of the cave, herded ahead by McQueen. Twilight lay deep, and first stars showed. When all three had clambered down the shale slope, McQueen drove his prisoners into the thicket where he'd left his horse and hung the two gun-belts over his saddle-horn. He mounted and accompanied first Duke to his picketed horse and then Buckner to where the livery-stable animal had been hidden out.

Buckner said then, "You don't need to stick to us like glue. If we're going through the gulch, we're going together, regardless. It's the three of us against Hatchet now."

Duke said, "We'll go through their camp like something shot out of a cannon."

But McQueen chose the wary approach. He herded the two single file ahead of him, Buckner up front, as they followed the windings of the gulch trail. McQueen still held his gun.

After a while, Buckner began wondering how McQueen had come upon the cave. Had he found the tracks of the horse Duke and Dorcas had ridden and followed them, or had some instinct of the professional manhunter served him? It didn't matter. Point was that McQueen had got there, and thus Duke was a prisoner now, and so was he because he had chosen to side Duke. He had waited at the cave in anger for Duke and ended up partner to Duke, and that was ironic until he thought again of the letter placed in Pru's hand.

He remembered Dorcas's impatience to be on her way, and it struck him then why Dorcas had been so eager. That letter, of course! Dorcas was hoping to keep the letter from being delivered. For a mile he meditated on how much it mattered to him whether Granville Cross got Duke's confession, and he didn't know; he only knew that in writing the letter Duke had done all that was possible to square for what had happened. He shook his head, thinking of Duke's planting that money in his bunk and of Dorcas's explanation of why Duke had done that. An account ruled closed. Everybody, he supposed, had an account needing closing. And then, strangely, he thought of Spence Rigby, him with the hangtree fever.

"Ease up," McQueen said, low voiced.

Darkened thicket and starlit winding of the trail had had a sameness to them. Buckner now saw they had come farther than he had supposed. Just ahead the gulch widened to meadow openness, and in the meadow a fire burned and horses moved and a tent stood, and near the fire were the figures of four—no, five—men, for here was Hatchet's camp.

Now there was room for the three to ride abreast, and McQueen whispered something, and Duke moved up stirrup to stirrup beside Buckner. McQueen moved up, too, and sat his saddle. "Slow and easy does it till they make a play," he decided. He frowned. "Trouble with being the law is you've got to hold tight till somebody else starts the trouble." He jogged his horse, and again they moved forward at a walk, heading across the meadow, each step of their mounts bringing them closer to the five. One of these crouched by the fire; the others were unsaddling. The one by the fire was Rigby, and it was he who spied the three first.

He raised no yell, flung no command to the others. Nearest Rigby was Rufe York, Buckner guessed from the bulk of the fellow; but with the firelight so feeble, he could only be sure of Rigby and his yellow slicker. Rigby darted toward a rifle leaning against a pile of gear. There would be no parley, no wordy defiance of the law. Rigby had recognized them and knew Duke to be one of them, and Rigby got to the rifle and brought it up. Flame broke from the Winchester, and the crash of the gun bounded from the gulch walls, bounced back and forth in echo.

"Run for it!" McQueen urged.

"My gun!" Buckner shouted at him. "Give me my gun! You'll get it back once I'm free of Hatchet!"

For a second McQueen hesitated. No reading that face, lost in shadow beneath the hat brim. Then McQueen plucked a gun from one of the belts looped over his saddle-horn and sent it sailing through the air. Buckner caught it. The three charged forward, thundering straight across the meadow.

Rigby, down on one knee, levered the rifle, firing shot after shot. Too angry to aim, Buckner judged; the bullets were a wild storm scattered everywhere. But the other Hatchet hands, caught up in the contagion of excitement, were firing, too. The meadow became an explosion of sounds. One of the men fought to get a saddle back onto a pitching horse. Few of Hatchet's crew were here. Where, Buckner wondered, were the others? Converging upon the camp with the sun gone? Would the trail be blocked even if he and Duke and McQueen made it into the timber?

They swept past the place where Buckner, listening to Tull and Rigby, had lain hidden last night. Duke hit the thicket first and sent his horse along the trail leading through it. McQueen swung after him. Rigby still fired, the bullets clipping through the trees. Buckner followed McQueen; but with the timber closed around him, he swung down from his saddle, hauled at the reins, and dragged his horse into a clump of bushes. He tied the mount securely. McQueen brought his own horse around and came back toward Buckner.

"Get on!" Buckner cried. "They'll be coming after us. And they've got re-mounts, fresher horses than ours. I'm staying to slow them. Don't argue! Get Duke down the hill!"

This time McQueen did no hesitating. He lifted the empty-holstered gun-belt from his saddle-horn and tossed it to Buckner, then wheeled his horse and headed on west. Buckner heard the dwindling beat of hoofs as McQueen and Duke put distance behind them. Duke would want to turn back, he guessed; but Duke would have no choice, not with McQueen still in command. A nearer sound drew his attention, the beat of hoofs coming from Hatchet's camp.

He ran back down the trail toward the meadow, the gun-belt looped over his arm. From the edge of the timber, he saw three men, Rigby one of them, up into saddles and charging across the openness toward him. Two others struggled to get saddles onto horses. He fired, and one of the three riders shouted in pain and clutched at his arm and turned aside. He fired again and again, not trying to aim but only to make it hot for Hatchet, to drive them back. They broke before his barrage and then spilled from saddles and took to the shelter of the bigger rocks strewn about.

He could hear them calling to each other, and one fired, the bullet coming close. He dove from the trail into the underbrush and began worming through it, pulling himself by his elbows. Rigby's voice reached him. Rigby was trying to urge the others to a rush, and a shard of speech came clear: ". . . only one of them . . ." Rigby sounded hysterical. Buckner kept working on through the brush until he could peer from it into the meadow. He saw a couple men rise from behind sheltering rocks and come running at the timber, bending low. He fired at them, and then the gun clicked empty.

He fumbled shells out of the belt and began reloading. He worked feverishly, awkwardly. Sweat came down into his eyes, blinding him. And then somewhere close by another gun opened from the thicket, the blaze of it turning the two Hatchet hands back. Buckner, astonished, peered in the direction of his ally. He could not see the man. Duke? McQueen? One or the other come back to side him? But Duke had been disarmed, and McQueen would be engaged in no such foolish heroics. He heard the crash of brush as his unseen friend came working toward him. Gulley Jordan's whisper reached him. "It's me! Don't go pluggin' me for a Hatchet hand!"

"Here, Gulley!" he whispered. "This way."

Gulley came crawling beside him. The old man punched fresh cartridges into his gun and then peered out into the clearing. "Seems they've lost their stomach for charging," he said.

Argument, blurred by distance, rose from the meadow. Buckner strained his ears. Rigby, trying to talk his men into rushing the thicket again, was making no headway. Someone—the voice sounded like Abe Lofstrum's—said, "There's two of them for sure, likely three. They're under cover, but we're naked if we move."

Buckner whispered to Gulley, "I figured you'd show hours ago, but at the cave, not here."

"You figgered wrong," Gulley whispered back. "Everybody else—Hatchet, you, McQueen, that girl—everybody wanted to get to Duke. That wasn't my notion. I just wanted to put myself where I could protect Duke if it got too hot for him. His biggest danger had to be Hatchet. I been here since mid-morning. I saw McQueen go up the gulch and later Duke and that girl, and then I saw the girl come back. Rigby and his men showed soon after that. Then you and Duke and McQueen came. That's when the lid blew off. I loaded a gun yesterday. Seemed the time had come to empty it."

"McQueen's taking Duke on to town."

"I figgered that," Gulley said. "It gave me a choice. Go after McQueen and see if I could get Duke away from him, or stay here and side you. But if it was you here in the brush, it meant you were staying back to cover for the others. That made you the one really needing help. That's the way I saw it."

Buckner nodded, knowing what such a choice must have cost Gulley. "I'm obliged," he said.

"Hey, McQueen!" Spence Rigby suddenly called from out there in the meadow. Buckner looked that way. Rigby was standing up, his fists raised to the sky, an easy shot for either man in the thicket. Gulley growled deep in his throat and raised his gun, but Buckner laid a hand on his arm.

"McQueen!" Rigby called again. "I know you're out there. Listen to me! You've got your man, and I can't budge these yellow pups to risk a run at you. You win this round. But I'll be following you to town as soon as my full crew is here. I'll take Jordan from you if I have to tear down the courthouse brick by brick to get at the jail section! Do you hear?" The rest of it was a wild rant, obscene, hysterical, incoherent.

"Crazy!" Gulley breathed, awed. "Crazy as a loon!"

"No," Buckner said. "Crazy as a fox, I think," for, listening to Rigby, his mind had gone back to that fragmentary thought he'd had about Rigby just before he and Duke and McQueen had reached the meadow; and from that, his thinking had shuttled to last night and Tull and Rigby talking out yonder. And a question had risen in him now, nagging and insistent.

He tugged at Gulley. "Let's get out of here."

"I've got my horse hid back a piece," Gulley said. "I'll meet you on the Bellafonte road."

"Keep your head down," Buckner said. He eased away, moving carefully, silently, to where he'd tied his own horse. He could still hear Rigby shouting wildly as he worked along. He mounted and got through the rocky slot that debouched upon the road, meeting no one on the way. He walked his horse downhill until presently Gulley loomed up behind him.

"To town?" Gulley asked. "McQueen's got too much start for us to catch up with him short of Signal. Me, I intend to be around when Rigby starts pulling the courthouse down."

"I leave you when we hit the valley," Buckner said. "When you see McQueen, tell him I said I'd hand back my gun once I was free of Hatchet. That time hasn't come quite yet."

"This road should be clear," Gulley said. "Even with half of them still out. They'll mostly be prowling back trails where Duke might have been."

"It's not stray Hatchet hands I'm thinking of," Buckner said, but he could say no more, even though Gulley and he now rode allied. How could a man put into sensible words a thing only felt and not truly known, a thing made of little pieces of knowledge and hunch, with some last ones yet to be fitted? He only knew where he must go and what he sought, for at last he had glimpsed why Spence Rigby was so set on seeing Duke Jordan hanged. Proving it would be another matter, but the proof might be the saving of Duke.

16 ⋮ To Hatchet

They came riding into the valley together, no man having risen out of darkness on the mountain road to block their way. Gulley had guessed right about that, Buckner conceded. He thought of all the riders moving across the face of the land. Somewhere ahead would be Dorcas, quirting hard for Signal, he judged; and on that same trail McQueen would be spurring, Duke with him. On the mountain to which they had put their backs, Hatchet hands gathered in Timmerman Gulch to feel the lash of Spence Rigby's fury. Riders everywhere, like so many puppets pulled by the strings of chance. A sense of excitement grew in him.

Half a horse ahead of Gulley, he pulled up where the road forked with ruts leading east toward Signal, ruts heading north to where Hatchet lay, and Boxed J. He sat his saddle feeling done in, the aftermath of that excitement in the gulch hitting him. His wounded shoulder hurt from having hauled himself through the brush. He hadn't been aware of his shoulder while the fuss was on, but now it was a dull, persistent ache.

Gulley drew up beside him. "Would it be Hatchet where you're headin'?" Gulley asked.

"Right," he said. "But I ride it alone, Gulley. You'd better go on to town as you planned."

Gulley looked thoughtful in the starshine. "You made peace with Duke, or you wouldn't have been hangin' behind to keep the wolves off his back." He hesitated. "You wouldn't be sayin' which one of you it was should have done that jail stretch?"

Buckner shook his head. "That's private between me and Duke."

Gulley fingered his saddle-horn and kept his eyes lowered. "If it was Duke should have gone to prison, I'd figger you had coming the amount of that cattle money that was supposed to have been stolen. I'd feel Boxed J owed you that, seein' you paid the price for having took it."

"The money never mattered one damn, Gulley."

"Still, the thing's got to be squared."

"It has been, Gulley." He lifted his reins. "So long now."

He headed his horse along that road to the north, bringing the mount to a gallop. When he looked back, Gulley still tarried at the turn, looking after him, a lumpishness in the night. When he glanced back a second time, several minutes later, Gulley was heading east, riding hard.

He let his own mount fall to a walk then. He had asked too much of the horse today. He peered toward Pothook, not far away but hidden by a fold of the valley floor. He could go to Pothook for a fresh horse, but doing so would lengthen the miles, and he had only the width of the valley to cross to Hatchet. Riding slowly on a tired horse might get him there as fast as side-tracking to get a fresh mount. He made his choice and rode on. He kept his eyes on the low hills ahead, the northern wall of the valley, and grew impatient, for those hills seemed to draw no nearer. He put his mind to other things, sorting over those little pieces of knowledge and hunch, keeping busy at this while the miles fell behind; and at last he crested a rise and looked upon Hatchet.

The ranch lay below him, a cluster of dark buildings with the northern hills a blurred backdrop. To his right, to the east, a few miles distant lay the Strip of ancient dispute; and farther to his right and almost to Signal lay Boxed J. He studied Hatchet as a soldier might study an enemy fort, his eyes moving from ranch-house to barn to bunkhouse to corrals to the several small out-buildings. One of these showed dim lamplight at a window. The cook-shack, he guessed, but wasn't sure; for Hatchet had been the enemy when he'd ridden for Boxed J and so was a place seldom seen. He put his horse down the slant and rode across level ground; and out of the prairie night a rider suddenly loomed.

This rider had come from that cluster of buildings and been lost in shadow before. The rider had to be an enemy; and there was no concealing himself now, not with the two of them nearly face to face. He got out his gun and said sharply, "Hold it!" and Pru's voice reached him, crying, "Ry? Is that you, Ry?"

She came out of her saddle and stumbled toward him. She said shakily, "I thought I recognized your voice. Oh, Ry!"

He thrust the gun away and stepped down from his

horse, and Pru fell into his arms. She shuddered and pressed close against him, and he heard himself saying soft, consoling things to her, but all the while his brain was whirling. What in the name of sense had brought her here? Then he realized that she was telling him, the story coming in little gasps of speech which had to be fitted together. Something about Dorcas and a fight over a letter and Pru fleeing with the letter, hoping to find Granville Cross here at Hatchet. Suddenly he understood.

"Duke's confession!" he said. "You fought Dorcas for it? You did that for my sake?" He was overwhelmed by this and touched as not even Duke's telling him of the letter had touched him. He held her closer, saying, "My dear. My dear."

She had pressed her face against his shoulder, and her voice came muffled. "I missed Granville," she said. "There's nobody here but the cook, and he's very drunk. I managed to get it out of him that Granville had come, found Tull and the crew gone, and so gone on about some other errands. I—I didn't know what to do. And then you came."

He released her and took her by the hand and led her to a flat outcropping of rock. "Sit down," he said gently; and when she did, he seated himself beside her. She took the letter from her coat and handed it to him. "Better you keep this till we can get it to Granville," she said.

He stowed the letter in a pocket. Now it was his turn to talk, and he told her most of what had happened since he had left her at the Brewsters' place the day before. He recounted this as quickly as he could, sketching in the events.

"Then Duke's in jail by now," she said when he'd finished. "That's best, I think. Do you really suppose Spence Rigby will try to take him from jail and hang him?"

"Yes," he said. "Spence will try. Unless his little game can be blown sky-high. That's why I've come here."

She had got hold of herself now and shaken off the shock of her struggle with Dorcas, her wild flight from Signal, the disappointment at Hatchet, and the surprise of finding him here, faceless at first in the night. Her voice, he noticed, had become even. "I'm afraid I don't follow you," she said.

"Let me try to talk it out," he said. "It will straighten my thinking. I suppose I first glimpsed a light when Dorcas accounted for Duke's double-cross of five years ago by saying that Duke couldn't truly be free of what he'd done till he'd ruled the account closed. Turning that over in my mind later, I got thinking of Spence Rigby. Not long after that, I listened to Spence rant when he thought he'd lost Duke to the law. That's when I really got wondering. Now just what is it that Spence has on his conscience that's going to keep troubling him till Duke's dead and the matter is closed?"

"Something to do with Lark's death?" she ventured.

"It just about has to be that," he said. "Now let's go back to what I overheard early last night when I hid outside Hatchet's camp. Spence and Sam Tull talked as partners. They've been meeting on the sly for about a year, I gathered; and from their secret talks came a partnership, put down on paper but not yet signed and sealed. Spence and Lark hated each other, remember; yet as Lark's lone relative, Spence stood to inherit Hatchet if anything happened to Lark. And Tull always resented being a hired hand instead of an owner. Looks like Spence and Sam Tull made a deal. Get Lark out of the way and Spence would own Hatchet, and Sam Tull was to be cut in for half, for helping."

"Sounds reasonable," she said. "And it jibes with the way a pair like Spence Rigby and Sam Tull would work."

"Granted that, we can assume that the two of them were waiting their chance at Lark Rigby. But that chance could have been hard come by, Lark being a tough hand. Then Gulley fenced the Strip, and Lark said he'd tear down that wire by the end of the week. He set out to do it, too, Tull with him. Duke found them at it, and words led to guns, and Duke shot Lark dead. Or did he?"

"I see what you're getting at!" Pru interjected, excited. "You're thinking that Duke perhaps only wounded Lark and then ran for it, thinking Lark dead. And that, Tull, seeing opportunity, finished the job."

He nodded. "Tull could have told the Hatchet crew the same story he carried to the sheriff—that Duke had done for Lark. The crew certainly wasn't in on the plot —Tull and Spence were careful last night to be out of earshot of the others when they did their talking. To Spence, Tull had probably told the truth of what happened to Lark, the better to lay claim to what Spence had promised for helping. And from there on, Spence and Tull had had to act like Duke was the killer; and the Hatchet crew, loyal to Lark's memory, became tools to their hand. They started spreading a net for Duke—they had men at the depot—and they tried lining me up against Duke, figuring I had no love for Boxed J."

"Of course," she said. "And right away Spence must have talked of hanging Duke. He pretended to be the aggrieved brother out for vengeance."

"But that pretense was only part of what was driving Spence, girl. You see, Spence had really won once Lark was dead and the blame fixed on Duke. Spence needn't have given a hoot what happened to Duke after that. But like Duke five years ago—who had won once he got that carpetbag away from me—Spence, with his guilty knowledge, couldn't feel fully secure till the account was ruled shut. In his case, that could only be when Duke dangled. Maybe Spence didn't even think it out that clearly. But ever since Lark went down, the one drive in Spence had been to see Duke hanged. He admitted that loco spot to Tull last night. And he still has it."

She sighed. "Interesting guesswork, Ry. But it's only guesswork."

"I know," he said. "But there's one more point. Last night Tull told Rigby that maybe he, Tull, had learned a few tricks from Spence about fancy scheming. He hinted that he might have an ace in the hole to use against Spence. Later that night, somebody shot Tull. Not me, and not Duke; and Gulley wasn't at the right place to have had the chance, and neither was Dorcas, nor McQueen, likely. That boils it down to Spence Rigby. With Lark out of the way, he didn't need Tull any longer; and Tull was pushing him to file that partnership paper. One bullet in Tull's back and Spence got both halves of Hatchet."

"But still that other matter would be unchanged," Pru said. "His drive to see Duke hanged."

"And that's why I'm here," he said. "To see if the guesswork can be backed up with something solid. Now what kind of an ace would Tull have had? Something in writing, I hope, something to hold over Spence's head, a scrap of paper, maybe, mentioning his deal with Spence and how Lark Rigby really came to die. Tell me, do you know if Tull slept in the bunkhouse?"

"In the ranch-house, Ry. I know that from something that was said in the mercantile one day."

He stood up. "You wait here. I'm going to have a look in that house."

"I'll go with you," she said and stood up, too.

He shrugged. "I suppose it will be safe enough. Hatchet will be heading to Signal, not here, I'm guessing."

They mounted and walked their horses to the hitch-rail before the ranch-house and tied up. Buckner looked at the house, a long, low, sod-roofed relic of another day. He had never been inside the house. The blinds were drawn, he noticed. He studied the house and then turned and walked across the yard to the bunkhouse, Pru with him. He opened the door and stepped inside and stood listening. Empty. He came out and started toward the barn.

"Just want to be sure nobody's here but the cook," he said.

"One horse in the corral," Pru whispered.

He recognized the horse. Tull's mount of last night,

come drifting home and turned in by the cook, he supposed. There were other horses in stalls in the barn. He looked toward the loft ladder but decided against investigating the haymow. He came back by way of the cookshack. Its door was ajar, and he paused before it long enough to hear the heavy snores of the occupant. That would be the cook, left here to tend stock and now deep in drunken sleep.

He headed back to the ranch-house, Pru silent beside him. He tried the door and found it locked. That was an odd thing in range country. The sense of excitement returned to him and began growing. He stepped back from the door, cocked a shoulder, and rammed the door hard. It burst inward on his third try.

He lunged into a large room, the living room likely, a stifling place with its closed-off smell of dead air and ancient tobacco smoke; but there was also, strangely, the smell of green timber and fresh shavings. He moved forward in the darkness and almost fell over something. A sawhorse, it seemed. He backed away and decided to light a match. In its flare he saw a centering table with a lamp upon it. He got to the table just as the match sputtered out. He used a second to get the lamp burning.

"Have to risk this," he said to Pru, who stood in the doorway.

He adjusted the wick and looked about. It was indeed a sawhorse he had stumbled against. There was a second one, also, and some planks on the floor, and a heap of shavings. He saw a small plane and a hammer and a can filled with nails and a handsaw. He nodded.

"Looks like Lark's coffin was built right here night before last," he said.

Pru nodded, too. Her eyes were wide, and she was made prettier by excitement as she had been at the Brewster place when Tull had held them under siege. She looked around the room where discarded clothes lay flung across chairs or on the floor. She looked at a heap of burlap sacking in one corner and at the furniture, homemade, crude, hard used, and at a big fireplace naked of andirons and littered with charred sticks and ashes.

"What a boar's nest!" she said.

Three doors gave off this room. Picking up the lamp, Buckner crossed to the first door and opened it. It gave into a cubby-hole of a kitchen. He held the lamp high, took one quick look, and closed the door. He moved to another and admitted himself to a bedroom. Lark Rigby's? Or Sam Tull's? He set the lamp on a makeshift dresser. The bed was made, but the blankets were rumpled. On the dresser stood a small tintype, and when he held it close to the lamp, he saw that it was a picture of Lark Rigby and two other men. From Rigby's appearance, the picture seemed to have been taken about ten years before. This, then, was Lark's room.

He came out and closed the door and went to the last room. This was another bedroom, the blankets a wild jumble, the dresser top strewn with a few coins, a broken comb, a deck of cards, very greasy and thumbed. Setting down the lamp, he began going through the dresser drawers. He found shirts and underwear and sox, some laundered, some soiled. He searched quickly but thoroughly. He found no writing of any kind. He pulled the bedding to the floor. He peered under the bed.

He came out of Tull's room, drawing the door shut after him, and put the lamp on the table and shook his head in answer to Pru's unspoken question. He stood frowning thoughtfully, his lips pursed. He looked at the sawhorses and the shavings and the tools. "Pru," he said, "I wonder if Spence came out here night before last. I was on Bottom Street when the funeral procession came in yesterday morning. Spence was riding up front with Sam Tull."

"I had to get down to the mercantile very early that morning," she said. "Spence was in town; I saw him ride out to the west. He either joined the procession here or met it on the way and rode back with it."

"No chance for Spence to have searched Tull's room the night of Lark's death, then. Besides, Tull didn't hint about his ace in the hole till the next night. And no wake for Lark, it seems. Just a box and a trip to town and a hole in the cemetery."

Pru shuddered. "If Duke got him between the eyes with a forty-five slug, as I heard, he was no sight to see. Tull probably built the box, put him in it, and nailed down the lid."

He shook his head. "Nothing more to do here," he said. "I've wasted time. Better I'd gone straight on to Signal."

He moved to the table and bent to blow out the lamp. He straightened up abruptly. "Did you hear it?" he asked.

"Hear what, Ry?"

"I don't know. Some kind of sound. Very faint. A sort of drumming."

He picked up the lamp again. He had another look in Tull's bedroom and Rigby's. He glanced toward the kitchen door, hesitated, then walked over and opened it. He stepped into the kitchen and found Pru close behind him. Nothing here but a rusty range, a crude table and a couple of chairs, a sink and pump, some cupboards. He raised the lamp. Set in the floor was a trapdoor with a ring handle. He knew where that would lead, to a cellar beneath the house, a place for storing vegetables. Some ranch-houses had such cellars; some had root cellars beyond the building.

"Might as well have a look," he said.

He raised the trapdoor and saw the dark maw of the cellar and the ladder leading down. He handed the lamp to Pru. "I'll just be a minute," he assured her. He lowered himself through the opening and groped with a foot for the rung of the ladder. He wouldn't have needed to. This cellar was shallow enough that he could have dropped to its dirt floor. The smell of rotted potatoes was strong, and the musty smell of damp earth. He looked up at Pru. "Mighty dark down here," he said. "Hand me the lamp, will you?"

She bent to give him the lamp, and he reached up to take it. She could look across his shoulder into the depth of the cellar; and thus as the light fell there, she was the first to see what lay beyond. Her eyes went wide, and he thought she was going to faint. He moved quickly to get the wavering lamp from her hand. Then a scream burst from her shrill against his ears; and he turned and saw what she had seen.

17 : The Hangmen

McQueen, moving aimlessly from his littered living quarters to his littered office, came to an abrupt halt and told himself he'd better sit down. He'd made this back-and-forth trip maybe a score of times, pretty near wearing a track in the floor, he supposed. Jumpiness was a disease that grew on a man and got worse with the growing. Trouble was that everything and everybody was so damn' quiet the silence had become like a shout. Not a stir out there in the night-blanketed street, and not a stir from Duke Jordan, the lone prisoner in the jail section beyond the office. Not much of a stir from Gulley Jordan, either, seated by the unpainted table, a morose lump of a man, opening and closing his fists sometimes, a worried look on his heavy-beaked face.

McQueen called to him from the doorway. "Coffee?" he asked, just wanting to hear a spoken word.

Gulley shook his head.

"All law-abiding folks in bed but us, I reckon," McQueen said. "That time of night."

Gulley stirred. "Nobody asleep at the Frontier, Virg."

"But that crowd's so quiet," McQueen said. "That's what bothers me. Horses at the hitchrail when I went down the street an hour ago, and they were Hatchet horses. Men at the bar, and they're Hatchet hands. Plenty liquor getting poured, but nobody hooting and hollering, and no flaming speeches being made by Spence Rigby. But he's there. And he's not just resting after a hard day in the saddle."

"I told you about the speech he made to me and Ry, thinking he was shouting at you," Gulley said. "You damn' betcha he's not just resting!"

McQueen said, "I could go have another look."

"No need, Virg. When the trouble starts, it will come to your door. You won't have to go down to where it's startin'." Gulley raised his huge right fist and brought it down hard on the table top. "Why didn't I cut over north and get my Boxed J boys and fetch 'em in?" he exploded. "I'd have had time to do that three times over, the way this thing has dragged out. But I figgered Hatchet would come howling into town so close on your heels and Duke's that they could taste your dust. I figgered it would be better if there was one more gun here pronto than ten guns on the trail!" He smote the table again.

McQueen, seeing the table shiver to that fist, thought, *Why, he's as tight-drawn as I am!* He cleared his throat, wanting to point out to Gulley that there still might be time to get help from Boxed J. Jake Hollis at the livery, or any street wayfarer might carry a note to Gulley's crew, fetching them. But he didn't say this. He wanted the notion to come from Gulley, not from himself. There was that much pride left to give shine to the badge he wore.

Gulley, his outburst finished, had sunk deeper in the chair so that his chin was on his chest. "No concern of theirs," he said deep in his throat.

"Meaning your crew?"

Gulley nodded. "I made my choice back in the valley. I never called for help in my life, Virg, 'lessen it was in my sleep. I'm too old to change now, spite of what I said a minute ago. I hired my hands to herd my cattle, not to fish me and my kin out of fires of our own makin'. I pay 'em workin' wages, not fightin' wages. Do you get what I'm drivin' at?"

Ah, yes, I do, McQueen thought, and in that moment he was the loneliest man in the world looking at the second loneliest. Two old-timers. Two men who had lived by the code of another day, a code of self-reliance, and now they were stuck with their own outmoded ethics. And both of them had known fear, so both of them had tasted of temptation. Yes, there had been that business with Ry Buckner in this very room the other night; and he colored now, remembering to his shame how he had tried blackmailing Buckner into taking a deputy's badge, and how Ry had been astonished at the offer coming from a man who had never appointed a deputy. "You used to say you didn't want anybody in your way when trouble started," Ry had pointed out. And it had been true. It had been so infernally true that now, like Gulley, when he needed to cry for help, he didn't know the words, having never learned them.

That was why he had paced from living quarters to office since getting back here, for he knew the danger and had nothing to pit against it but himself and Gulley, two old men slowed by the years but holding to pride because there was nothing else left.

Two, three hours now since he had ridden in and locked Duke in a cell and waited alone till Gulley had come here to tell of Spence Rigby's hysterical threat. Gulley had sat at the table since, not even having a look in at Duke. Hadn't wanted to see his boy behind bars, McQueen had figured, and could understand that part of pride, too. He'd left Gulley holding the fort and taken the one turn up and down the street and found Hatchet liquoring at the Frontier and known what that boded.

The rest of the time had been frittered at waiting, and all this while he might have been out pounding doors. He might have enlisted the town, man by man, telling them he faced a thing too big for him and asking that they throw a ring of guards all around the courthouse. Even an Oliver Landers was not so small but what he could tote a rifle. But he hadn't gone after Landers or anyone else because, like Gulley, he had no voice for calling for help.

And there was another thing holding him back. You were elected sheriff term in and term out, and you drew your salary from taxpayers' money, and the job was some different from the town-taming Kansas days. Maybe you had to arrest a Saturday night drunk or see about a stolen saddle or talk a man into muzzling his dog, but mostly you roundsided in your office or walked the street looking stern, living off the fat of your reputation. You were like a fireman in one of the big cities, playing cards or petting a spotted dog or currying the horses to keep them sleek against the hour when the gong rang and the harness dropped into place and you were off to the smoke and the danger. Twenty-nine days out of a month you drew your pay for doing nothing, but on the thirtieth day you might be expected to earn it. And that was why, when the gong sounded, you couldn't go to the taxpayer and ask him to jump on the wagon with you and ride to where the blaze bannered. You had taken on a job, and it was nobody's concern but yours; and that fact, too, became a part of pride.

"Coffee—?" he again asked Gulley.

Gulley lifted his head, but not to the question. "Somebody rattlin' the office door, I think."

McQueen heard the sound, too. He stepped into the office and crossed it to the street door and stood to one side, drawing his gun. "Who's there?" he demanded.

"Dorcas. Please let me in."

He slid back the bolt and admitted her, then quickly bolted the door again. Only then did he pouch his gun. She blinked in the lamplight. He had expected no peaceful visitor at this late hour, and his face must have showed his surprise. "I'm sorry to bother you," she said. "I went to bed and tried to sleep, but I couldn't. You've got Duke here now?"

He nodded.

"I'd like to see him, if I may."

He gestured with his head toward the jail section, and she walked into the corridor which gave off this office from the side opposite his quarters. He stood waiting. He could hear the murmur of her voice and Duke's, but he could not make out the words. Still, he began to feel like an eavesdropper, so he went back to the other room and sat down at the table across from Gulley.

"What's *she* want?" Gulley asked with open antagonism.

He didn't bother answering. Presently Dorcas appeared in the doorway. She looked disheveled and tired and woebegone, yet she looked strangely at peace with herself. She did not so much as nod to Gulley.

"I walked along Bottom Street before I came here," she said. "Hatchet's at the Frontier. I suppose you know that."

"Yes," McQueen said.

"I'd like to wait here with you," she said. "Even if it means staying up all night."

Gulley said with both anger and alarm, "You go home, girl!"

Dorcas shook her head. "Duke and I were married this afternoon. My place is here. I promise I won't be in the way if—if they come."

Gulley sat bolt upright. "You and Duke married—!" His face began working so that it looked as though he were crying. McQueen, watching him, judged that until this moment Gulley had not liked this girl but that whatever he had based his dislike upon had proved to be a shadow without substance. It was as though Gulley had long looked at one Dorcas only to find now a different one; and plainly he was deeply moved by this discovery and even gladdened.

"Married!" Gulley said dazedly. "Girl, I had it figgered you'd told Virg, here, where to find Duke. I read the sign all wrong." He raised his eyes to McQueen. "Let her stay, Virg. Like she says, she belongs here."

McQueen got up and fetched another chair to the table for Dorcas. When she had seated herself, Gulley looked down at his big hands, opening and closing them again. "You'll have to give me time to get used to the idea, girl," he finally said. "I never had a daughter."

That was when Dorcas smiled. "And I never had a father," she said.

They sat, the three of them, in silence. They sat, while somewhere in the cluttered area of cot and brick-propped kitchen range and lumpy sofa a clock ticked relentlessly. McQueen's mind turned to Ry Buckner, who'd ridden to Hatchet on some mysterious mission, according to what Gulley had reported. He wished Buckner would show here; and then he thought, annoyed, *What the hell difference would one more man make?* Buckner was just so many pounds of bone and gristle, the same as anyone else. On the other hand, there was something more to Buckner, and he began wondering how that could be.

He thought of Duke Jordan, a fugitive up until a few hours ago; and he thought of all the pursuers, Buckner among them; and he knew the difference then. With one exception, it had been the pursuers who were really pursued—himself by the fear of showing that crack in his armor, Dorcas by her ambition, Gulley by his concern over Duke, Tull by his dark brutality, Spence Rigby by that virulence, hangtree fever. Only Ry Buckner had ridden as a free man, wanting no more than to reclaim a friendship, wanting nothing for himself, really, wanting only to believe in Duke Jordan again. That was what made Buckner formidable, his being free of selfishness, his being unpursued. And that was why he wished Ry Buckner were here now in this hour of need.

This thinking gave him a glimpse of something else that he struggled to grasp, but his mind was sluggish from long worry. Then he got hold of it. Forget yourself, and you forgot fear. Forget the personal man that was you, the personal needs, and you could stand straight as a rifle and as unbending! Odd, but he had known that long ago, in his youth, and then forgotten. But it was worth recalling.

He was wrenched from thought by the alert look on Gulley's face, and at the same time he heard what Gulley heard, the knock on the street door. He got up and again went to the door and drew his gun as he stood to one side. "Who is it?" he asked.

"Me. Rufe York. Let me in."

"You alone?"

"Just me. Come under a flag of truce, you might say. Let me in."

He slid back the bolt and saw the door give to York's hand, and all the while he held the gun ready. There was no one crowded behind York, no pack of Hatchet hands out there in the street. York stood in the office teetering slightly, more than a little drunk, and the lamplight gave a hard shine to his eyes. McQueen shut the door and bolted it. "All right, Rufe," he ordered, "get it said."

York took a couple of steps forward and so was able to see into the room where Gulley and Dorcas sat. Finding Dorcas here astonished him. He shook his head, plainly not liking this. Then he said, "I was sent to make a speech. I'll make it short. We're comin' after

Duke. You could make it a heap easier for yourself, Virg, by just handin' him over to us."

McQueen said, "I'm not about to do that. Show some sense, Rufe. You know better than to be mixed up in this, and so do the rest of the Hatchet boys. Get them together and take them home. Whatever Duke's got coming the law will deal out to him."

York had been prepared for this. His stubbornness showed in the shake of his head. "In a court it's who's got the most expensive lawyer to do the fastest talkin'. A rope's a lot quicker and surer. Lark Rigby was our boss, Virg. We drew his pay, and we ate his grub. The way it was told to us, Lark didn't have no chance."

"Tull's say-so, Rufe. If it's worth anything, it will stand up in court."

"Not with Sam dead," York said. "That's the clincher that makes what Spence wants done what we want. Sam wasn't of much account, and I've done no weepin'; but just the same Sam didn't rate himself any bullet in the back."

"Sam dead?" McQueen said and felt stunned. Nobody had told him Tull had been shot, yet it was as though he had expected such news. When he had tried bargaining with Buckner and later bargained with Dorcas, he had been trying to head off trouble, knowing how it grew. You started with one dead man, Lark Rigby, and now there was another, Sam Tull, and you wondered where the killing would end.

"Plumb dead," York said. "A couple of our boys, comin' in late from huntin' Duke, stumbled onto Sam after sundown and fetched him to Timmerman Gulch.

That was after you and Duke and Buckner had gone through us. Sam won't be tellin' his story in court against Duke, and that makes the best reason of all why we ain't waitin' for Duke to get to court. Now you'd better make it easier for yourself, Virg."

"Go home, Rufe. Go home and take your crew with you. You threw bullets at me in Timmerman, but I'm forgetting that. You come here as a hangman, it's a different matter."

"We got men," York said. "About a dozen of us. We got guns and the cause to use 'em, and we've got a length of old telegraph pole to make a batterin' ram that will go through that door of yours like a match through soft butter. You won't stand a chance, Virg."

McQueen stepped to the door and slid back the bolt and opened the door with his free hand, temper strong in him as the sap of youth. "Get out of here, Rufe. Get out before I forget that flag of truce you're supposed to be carrying and boot your rump into one of the empty cells."

York looked into the next room, looked at Dorcas. "You go home, girl. Right away. Hear?"

Dorcas did not look up at him or answer.

York turned about and headed for the street door, staggering a little, and stepped outside. McQueen bolted the door behind him. He dropped his gun back into its holster and came to the doorway of his quarters and stood there, the words running in his mind to order Dorcas home. They stayed unsaid. She would not go, and he knew it.

He could hear that clock hammering on. He searched

with his eyes for the clock; it must be midnight or past by now. He remembered he'd found the clock run down when he'd come back here tonight and he'd wound it and set it by guess. What matter what time it was, anyway? Five minutes, ten minutes, fifteen minutes this side of doomsday.

Gulley lifted his head. "Listen!" he said.

McQueen could hear them, too, their boots shuffling out there on the street. They were not coming with yells and shouts; they had no wish to arouse a town that might stand beside the law whether asked or not. The amateur firemen who always showed to clutter up a scene of conflagration.

"Dorcas," he said sharply, "you stretch out on the floor face down. And stay there till it's finished. Understand?"

"I can handle a gun," she said.

"On the floor," he insisted. "That's my order."

He turned back into his office and went to a rifle rack and took down a Winchester and tested the lever action. He found Gulley beside him. Gulley stood straight, no fear showing on him, and he wondered if Gulley understood that within the next few minutes they'd likely both be dead. He wondered if he looked as unconcerned as Gulley. And then he knew that such must be so, for he was done with fear. That had come from thinking about Ry Buckner. Forget yourself, and you forgot fear.

He jerked his head toward the rifle rack. "Help yourself, if you're so inclined," he said to Gulley. Outside that shuffle of boots came closer and closer, with

Hatchet almost to the door. He ran his hand along the straight barrel of the rifle. "A revolver is maybe better for close work," he said, "but I rather fancy this tonight. There's something about a rifle I like."

18 : Showdown at Signal

Buckner had stood stock still in Hatchet's cellar, the lamp in his hand and Pru's scream rising until he said sharply, "Get hold of yourself!" She ceased screaming as abruptly as though he had slapped her.

"Sorry, Ry," she said. "Too much today, I guess." She let herself onto the ladder and came down to a stand close to him and looked to one side of the cellar. She shuddered. "I could only see his boots before. He's dead, isn't he?"

"No, Pru," he said. "He's got to be alive. That's what makes him Tull's ace in the hole."

Yet Lark Rigby looked more dead than alive, propped up with his back to the dirt wall, his legs thrust out before him. A light chain, fastened about one of his ankles, ran to a post supporting the floor above and was secured by a padlock. A blood-stained bandage made a turban around his head; his face was caked with grime and blood; and only his eyes were alive, regarding them glassily. Fear dwelt in his eyes, and defiance, too, and the great question: *Who are you?*

Then Rigby knew, for Buckner was holding the lamp so that the light fell on him and Pru; and Rigby said, "Water—!" in a harsh, croaking voice.

Potatoes were heaped here, and some cased canned goods, these things beyond Rigby's reach because of the shortness of the chain. Buckner placed the lamp on top of one of the cases and said to Pru, "Get him some water, will you. Quick!" Pru went back up the ladder. Buckner moved to Rigby and knelt beside him. A tin can lay near Rigby. It had held water once, but it was empty now. "Easy," Buckner said. "It will just be a minute." He could hear Pru working the pump at the kitchen sink above. "Don't try to talk," he cautioned Rigby.

Pru came back into the cellar carrying a pitcher of water. Under her arm she had a stale-looking loaf of bread she had located somewhere. She handed the pitcher to Buckner, and he held it to Rigby's lips. The man sucked in the water in great, noisy gulps; some of it ran down his shirt front. Buckner pulled the pitcher away from him, and Rigby fought feebly to hang onto it. "More!" he croaked.

Buckner thrust the loaf of bread at him instead, and Rigby seized this and tore away a chunk and crammed it into his mouth. Buckner gave him the rest of the water then, and Rigby drank this and wolfed more of the bread. He said then in a voice much more his own, "He left me a little grub and a can full of water, but that's long gone. How long? A day—a week? Nothing but night down here, around the clock, and nobody stirring in the house until you came. It's Ry Buckner, ain't it? Heard you were out. And Prudence Lane."

"We nearly missed you," Buckner said. "We nearly left without looking into the cellar."

"I could hear you moving around. First I thought it was Sam come back. Then I made out there was two of you, and I began hoping you might be a couple of the crew. Sam hadn't let the crew in on this, so there was a chance you two might be good news. I was too dry to do any shouting, so I drummed against the post with my feet, still not sure whether I might be fetching friend or enemy. Have you any idea how long I've been down here?"

"Probably since night before last, Lark. You say you expected Sam back. That means you know he put you here."

Rigby nodded. "This started with a run-in I had with Duke Jordan at the Strip fence. Sam was with me, and Duke used a gun on me. Ah, I see by your faces you both know about that. Duke's bullet must have creased the top of my head. I remember the blood blinding me; then I pitched into a black hole a million miles deep. Next thing I knew, I was on my bed upstairs. Sam was standing there looking at me, his face like a wolf's. He'd bandaged my head. I remember lifting my hand and feeling the bandage. Then I fell into that black hole again. Seems I remember some sawing and hammering going on in the house, but maybe I dreamed that. Next thing I knew, I woke up to find myself chained down here, with nobody home upstairs and nobody within shouting reach."

"Sam brought you home unconscious," Buckner explained. "He must have told the crew you were dead and no sight to see. He built you a coffin and put something in it for weight—iron, likely, wrapped in burlap sacking to keep it from rattling. The andirons are gone from the fireplace, and I suppose there were other scraps around. He nailed the coffin shut, and everybody supposed it was holding you. Truth was, Tull wanted you dead. He'd been scheming with Spence, the deal being that if you died and Spence inherited, Sam would be half-owner here."

"Spence, eh?" Rigby said, his face wooden in the lamplight. "Spence crossed my mind while I was spending time here thinking. He fits. Sam wasn't sharp enough for that kind of scheming."

"Sharp enough to have learned from Spence, though," Buckner said. "Sharp enough to see that if he made you look dead but kept you alive a few days, he'd have Spence over a barrel if Spence tried reneging on that partnership deal."

"How do you know so much about this?" Rigby demanded. "Never mind. That can wait. Get this chain off me. I want to find Sam Tull and have a few words with him."

"Sam's dead, Lark. As it shapes up, it had to be Spence who killed him, to dissolve the partnership. You see, Spence, thinking you dead and buried, has had the Hatchet crew on Table Mountain chasing Duke Jordan. Last night Sam left their camp to go prowling. As I see it now, his prowl would have brought him back here where he'd have given you some more food and water to keep you alive a bit longer. You were to have stayed alive till Sam could safely let go of his ace. Then Sam would have put you out of the way. As it happened, Spence might have done for you by starvation, when he put a bullet in Tull. That bullet could have been your finish, if someone hadn't come soon and found you."

"I'll be seeing Spence," Rigby said grimly.

"He'll be in Signal, Lark. Trying to drag Duke out of jail where McQueen put him tonight. Spence can't figure his little game finished till Duke dies for killing you."

"Then let's get riding," Rigby said. "There should be a horse or two left around the place, and I've got a gun I keep hid out in the barn. Let's go see Spence. Will you get this damn' chain off me?"

Buckner nodded. Rigby seemed nearly restored by food and water and anger to the man remembered from other days, a man smaller than Spence in build but with something solid to him, a man of quick temper and forceful action. A man who had made a formidable enemy and could be a stalwart friend. He ran his eye from the chain about Rigby's ankle to the padlock that fastened it. The key would be wherever Tull had put it, probably in his pocket. Buckner lifted out his gun and blasted at the padlock, the explosion filling the cellar. When the smoke drifted, the lock lay shattered. He disengaged the chain and helped Lark Rigby to stand up.

They hit Signal near midnight, riding hard all the way, the three of them pounding stirrup to stirrup on Hatchet horses, Rigby having loaned Pru and Buckner replacements for their tired mounts. They had skirted the Strip where Gulley Jordan's barbed wire glinted in the starshine; they had come past Boxed J and glimpsed its lighted bunkhouse from a distance. Buckner had thought then of the crew that might be called to ride with them, but there was no need for extra help. Sight of Lark Rigby would turn Hatchet from its purpose, for the crew had no such compulsion to a hanging as drove Spence Rigby, and the excuse would be gone with a dead man come alive. They had galloped hard across the last miles, through the broken country of rock and bluff and stunted tree, riding into the moon that lifted out of the east. And so they rode into Bottom Street.

The only splash of light fell from the Frontier, and the hitchrail was lined with horses, most of them bearing the Hatchet brand; but as they went past, Buckner looked in and saw that the saloon was deserted. Lamplight shone on bare table and empty chair and vacated bar. He knew then where Hatchet had liquored and where Hatchet had gone. *Too late?* he wondered and looked on up the street toward the courthouse.

They still rode in full career. He saw Lark Rigby to his left, bent low over the horn, his hat brim flattened back, his face grim and white. Rigby was going on sheer nerve, Buckner knew. He turned his gaze to Pru, at his right, and wondered if he should tell her to leave them now, but he judged that she wouldn't be so inclined. She had been steadfast and so earned the right to see the finish, and he could only hope there would be no danger for her.

They had had no time for talking on this hard ride. He had got in a few more words with Lark while they had saddled in Hatchet's barn; he had sketched in the situation quickly for Lark, telling him what had happened on the mountain these last two days. They had no time for talking now.

They hit the courthouse corner and swung right and

saw the dark mass of men on the side street like bees clustered on a branch, for they were carrying a length of telegraph pole, moving this ram toward the door leading into McQueen's office. The queer thing was their silence. Buckner shook his head, feeling as though he had gone deaf. No wild shouting here, no noisy threats. Only the silent night and the chalky moonlight and the double line of men rushing that ram forward.

Until the gun spoke.

He recognized that throaty cough as coming from a Winchester. McQueen or someone else inside was firing through the door; and at the shot, Hatchet fell back and Spence Rigby's voice lifted, urging them on. A couple of the crew had let go of the pole. They moved in again, taking their places; and that was when Lark Rigby hauled hard on his reins, bringing his horse to a sliding stop. Standing in his stirrups, he yelled, "Hatchet! Hold up!"

Buckner saw faces turn their way; he even saw the startled white of those faces. He heard someone shout in a voice made high and girlish by astonishment, *"My God! It's Lark!"* He saw the telegraph pole drop, and the door of McQueen's office open. McQueen stood there, peering out, drawn by that cry, a smoking rifle in his hand. Behind him stood Gulley Jordan, and looking over Gulley's shoulder was Dorcas. The lamplight falling through the open doorway touched Hatchet's crowded men, highlighting the gaping faces they turned toward Lark Rigby.

"Lark!" one shouted. "Is that sure as hell you, Lark?"

"Spence!" Lark Rigby called in a voice of thunder. "Come here, Spence!"

Spence Rigby had stood back from the others, big and recognizable in his yellow slicker. His round face showed the same astonishment as the others', but his held something else as well, fright that turned into fury. He started to run but swung back, his hand jerking open his slicker and bringing out a gun. Buckner thought frantically of Pru, here beside him and Lark Rigby. Spence tilted the gun toward his brother, but the explosion that filled the night came from another gun, in Rufe York's hand. Spence was carried backward as though by a great wind. His feet tangled, and he went down.

Buckner got off his horse and began fighting his way through Hatchet's crew. No man stopped him; they were no longer the enemy. He got to where Spence Rigby lay writhing, his gun fallen beside him. He kicked Spence's gun away. He knelt by Spence and found Lark Rigby come up, too. Lark stood looking down at Spence. Spence shook his head as though trying to clear his vision. "Tull, damn him—he did this," he said chokingly. "Double-crossed me—glad I killed him—" He was talking to nobody, but now he seemed to see Lark. "Sorry," he said. "Sorry." His eyes went vacant. "Tried hard—to get Duke Jordan—wanted to square for you—"

He died then. Lark turned away, and Buckner stood up and saw big Rufe York towering over his boss. Rufe had a whiskey smell about him, but he had become cold sober and looked as though he were going to be sick. He said, "Lark, you gotta know I didn't want to shoot.

He was your brother. But, hell, Lark, it was you or him—"

"I know that," Lark Rigby said gruffly. "I'll remember how it was, Rufe." He brushed on past York, walking like a man in his sleep.

Buckner, too, felt like a sleepwalker. He moved as if in a dream, some of it sharp, some of it fuzzy. He found himself in McQueen's office, and Pru was with him, and Lark, too. McQueen was here, and Gulley and Dorcas, and some of Hatchet's crew. Everyone seemed to be talking at once. There was a babble of questions and answers, with some things being said over and over again, what with people not quite understanding and wanting this or that point squared away so that it made sense that Lark was here alive. A few townspeople hurried in, drawn by the shots.

Buckner noticed after a while that the office door was open; and when he looked out into the street, Spence's body had been toted away. Presently the townspeople left one by one, and Hatchet was gone save for Lark, who now stood looking across the room at Gulley Jordan. Gulley was shaking his head as though he'd heard too much in one night and was trying to straighten everything out in his mind.

Lark said, "Gulley, there's one thing I want to say. I guess my mistake was in not knowing who really was my enemy. There'll be no more trouble over that Strip fence."

"Reckon not," Gulley said. "I'm tearin' it down tomorrow. We'll not need anything between us after tonight."

Buckner wandered into the jail corridor and then

wished he hadn't. Dorcas was here, standing before the one occupied cell, talking through the bars to Duke. Buckner came on until he, too, was before the door and could see Duke.

"Ry!" Duke said eagerly. "Some doings tonight! Dorcas has been telling me about Lark's showing up alive and how it was your thinking that took you to where he was. I'm mighty obliged, Ry."

"Sure, Duke," he said. He looked at these two, man and woman, thinking that they had both been very dear to him and always would be. But he had left them now, left them in Timmerman Gulch for that matter, for they moved in a world of their own, big enough for two but not for three. Yet he smiled, for the steadfast things were stored memories and the knowledge of faith kept, not only with people, who sometimes showed themselves not wholly worthy, but with himself. He remembered the letter then, and Dorcas's intent. He drew the letter from his pocket. A cuspidor stood here in the corridor. He tore the letter to bits and dropped these into the cuspidor.

"My wedding present to the two of you," he said. "You go confessing to Cross anyway, Duke, and you throw the gift back in my face. I wouldn't like that."

Dorcas said, "It's more than we deserve, Ry. Me, anyway."

Duke said in a voice not quite his own, "Ry, you and I have been a little too much on the move to get around to shaking hands." He thrust his hand between the bars.

Buckner shook his hand and then leaned and brushed his lips against Dorcas's cheek. "And a kiss for the bride," he said. "Here comes McQueen jangling his keys. He's finally remembered that there isn't a reason in the world why you should be locked up, Duke."

He turned away and passed McQueen in the corridor. He remembered McQueen as of earlier, flinging open the street door and standing there with the smoking rifle in his hand, a man doing his work; and he nodded respectfully at McQueen. He found the office deserted, but he glimpsed Gulley and Lark Rigby and Pru in McQueen's quarters, the three standing close together, talking. Someone had brought the coffee pot to the front of the stove, and it was beginning to bubble. He felt tired, and he wanted nothing so much as a breath of fresh air, so he opened the street door and slipped out . . .

He sat up here on the south slope, his back to the railroad track, sat with his knees drawn up and his arms locked around them; and from this crest he looked at the buildings of Signal below, formless in the depth of the gulch and along its slopes, the great bulk of the courthouse centering the town. He had sat here a long time; it would soon be dawn. He had done his thinking, and he was at peace with himself, for he knew where his destiny lay.

He stirred now, seeing someone toiling up the slope toward him; and he knew her—he knew Pru. He would never mistake her for Dorcas again, for he knew the difference.

She was panting when she reached him, and for a moment she simply stood before him, waiting to get her breath, and then she laughed. "I've searched the town over for you. I even woke up Jake Hollis to ask if you were in the livery loft. My, how that man can swear! Finally I remembered that the way you came back might be the way you'd leave. You great ninny! Don't you know there's no freight through here till night after next?"

"I'm not waiting for a train," he said. "I just came up here for a look."

"Where to, then, Ry?"

He waved his hand at the huddled buildings below and the valley beyond. "It's my town and my range," he said. "There'll be a place for me in it. Someday I'll get some land and a few cattle to stock it. Enough to make a start."

"Of course," she said. "We'll begin working for that land as soon as we get married."

He shook his head. "Pru," he said very seriously, "how could I offer you that? You'd remember me and Dorcas five years ago. You'd always think of yourself as second choice."

She sat down beside him. "First choice," she said. *"My* first choice—my only choice." She began laughing again, and he liked that; he remembered how she had laughed that night he'd crawled through the window at her house. He knew now that he had always liked her laughter. He had found laughter lacking in Dorcas, that and the joy of free living that belonged to those who went forth unharried to meet whatever the world might hold for them.

"Don't think me forward for asking you to marry me, Ry," Pru murmured. "You see, there's a lesson I learned from Dorcas, something she told me tonight—a couple of ages ago. She said that what you really want you should go after. It was a long, hard climb up here, Ry."

He put his arm around her and drew her close to him. "When you've rested," he said, "we'll walk back down together."